One Way Donkey Ride

One Way Donkey Ride

fiction by

MARK E. CULL

ASYLUM ARTS
PARADISE
2002

The following stories in this book have previously appeared in the following publications: *Dirigible*, "Something Like Jennifer;" *Webgeist*, "Prince of the Synagogue;" and the anthology *Anyone Is Possible* (Red Hen Press, 1997), "The Red Notebook."

Special thanks to Michael H. Boas, Peter Pryor and especially Karen Lewis.

Cover photograph by the author.

ISBN 1-878580-22-1
Library of Congress Catalog Card Number 00-134468

Printed in Canada.

FIRST EDITION

Asylum Arts
5847 Sawmill Road
Paradise, CA 95969

for
Kate

To be a man is to strive to be God

—*Jean-Paul Sarte*

Contents

One Way Donkey Ride

The Red Notebook

Old Orchard Road runs parallel to Main Street, beginning just behind the closed dairy, breaking for the drainage wash and then running the rest of the way to the other side of the freight yard just east of town.

It is the first week of kindergarten. José and Molly follow Cherry Avenue until it meets Old Orchard. This is the section of the road which passes just behind their school. They are only a block away from their normal path and José tells Molly that they will probably not be late. Nobody will know where they had been anyway.

It is with an odd sort of pride that José carefully steps through the charred remains of his grandfather's home. The fire had been the town's big event of the summer. All the volunteers were called in, but the house had long since burned to the ground by the time they arrived. The better half of the town watched as the house blazed away for nearly an hour. It was later discovered that the old man never made it out of bed. José lowers his voice while retelling this particular fact. Molly covers her eyes and begs him to stop. She does not want to hear another word. Molly has already heard far too many of the horrible details from her older sister. José begins to describe how his grandfather's body had been found. It is at this that Molly begins to scream wildly, and then runs toward the street with still covered eyes. In the distance a dilapidated rust-red pickup truck backfires as it lurches down Old Orchard. José dashes after Molly, grabbing her dress sleeve as she steps onto the cracked sidewalk.

"Stop or we'll get in trouble," he says pulling her to a stop.

"What trouble?" she asks uncovering her eyes. "You're saying stuff I don't want to hear."

"You'll get runned over and we'll be late to school. That's what trouble," José eyes the old truck as it slowly rolls by. Molly stares after its large black tires and then gives José a shove.

"You're stupid to go in the street José, my sister told me to only walk on the yellow line when cars *stop*."

"You're stupid, you're gonna get runned over," José points after the truck thinking how he should just hit her in the arm. He decides not to since she is a girl, and his father might find out. Instead, he grabs her by the hair and pulls her off the sidewalk. Molly shoves him again.

"You're stupid to always play in the street. *You're* gonna be runned over. You're the trouble," she says stepping back onto the sidewalk. Molly starts to walk toward school. José jumps over a crack in the sidewalk and lands on the narrow curbing next to the street.

"My brothers and I never get hit. Watch!" He shouts.

Molly looks back to see José performing a high wire act along the curb's edge. Turning back around she sees another car driving onto Old Orchard from Cherry Avenue.

"Car!" she shouts and looks back again to see José immediately dropping his outstretched arms and stepping back onto the sidewalk.

The advancing car seems to be moving far too quickly for such a narrow street. It is the sort of white convertible her sister calls a "sports" car. Molly looks into the car to see if its driver is someone she knows. Seemingly there is nobody behind the steering wheel as the car veers sharply from the center of the road toward the sidewalk just ahead of her. Before hitting the curb, a woman's head appears from the passenger side. The car immediately rights itself. Molly recognizes their kindergarten teacher, Miss Conejo.

The woman smiles and waves to Molly as her car rushes along the street. At this, Molly smiles to herself and skips cheerfully for a few paces. She is shocked by the screech of braking tires and spins about in time to see Miss Conejo's car swerve directly into the sidewalk and do a perfect somersault into the middle of the burned-out lot a short distance behind. The upside down wheels of the little white car spin madly for a moment as the engine roars. After a few moments, the engine fails and the rear tires jerk to a halt while the wheels in front continue to spin without change. From the middle of the street, José stares with his mouth wide open.

"Now we *are* in trouble!" Molly cries as José cautiously steps back onto the curb. Staring at the still spinning wheels, she feels incapable of deciding between running the rest of the way to school before getting into still more trouble or staying and taking a closer look at Miss Conejo's upturned car.

Molly and José stare in awe at the spinning wheels for nearly a minute. After the wheels slow and then finally come to a stop, José finds he is able to look around. The street is empty. Running to the upside down car, he attempts to open Miss Conejo's door. His brothers had told him that this was the sort of thing a gentleman does. José tilts his head sharply to one side in hopes that the proper perspective might be helpful. The door is obviously stuck.

As José makes a variety of unsuccessful attempts to open Miss Conejo's door, Molly slowly paces around the car in a wide arc, being careful to not get any closer than she already is. Stepping around the remains of a yellowed shattered commode, Molly's eyes are drawn to a bit of dark red coming out from under the car's passenger side door. Stepping closer, Molly recognizes the red notebook their teacher took attendance in the day before. Kneeling on the blackened ground she tries to pull the half-exposed notebook from under the car. It is clamped tightly between the white car door and a black pile of loose ash, refusing to move when pulled by the young girl. Molly wriggles the notebook from side to side for a few moments and then manages to pull it free.

Wrapping her small arms tightly around the now charcoal black and red notebook, Molly springs away from the car and runs as quickly as she can toward school. Nearing Cherry Avenue, she can hear the sound of José's feet close behind.

△

Unlike the well-known one room schoolhouse, the town's only school is relatively modern in design, and has enough students that from kindergarten through twelfth every grade has its own classroom. Like many of the larger schools, the kindergartners are separated from the rest of the children. The small ones' classroom and playground are isolated from the rest of the school by a chain link fence. They have their own street entrance in addition to an interior gate that opens near the main office. The town is small enough that is has not learned the sort of cynicism that closes windows at night or puts locks on gates.

Just as many children run through the kindergarten's open streetside gate as walk. A few of these runners have oddly imbalanced systems fueled by artificially sweetened meals. Some dash about so wildly that when Molly and José arrive breathless nearly five minutes before the school bell rings, they are barely noticed.

Once inside the gate, Molly skips over to the playhouse, next to the large sandbox, where her friends meet before the morning bell rings. José runs directly for the jungle gym.

When the bell rings, the children quickly form a line beginning just outside of the yellow arc painted on the ground near the classroom door. Since he and Molly walk together, José stood just behind Molly and her friends for the first few days of school. This morning he stands closer to the back of the line with the children who shove into each other laughing.

After a few minutes pass and Miss Conejo fails to appear from the classroom, even the children near the head of the line begin pushing each other. Molly looks for José and then dashes toward the back of the line once she sees him.

"Open the door," she whispers into his ear. José's eyes become wide as he shakes his head *No*. When his head finally stops shaking, Molly pushes him hard enough to make him trip as he steps backward. While the other children laugh at this, Molly runs past the head of the line and pulls the classroom door open. Molly disappears into the dark room, and in a few moments lights flicker on.

The kindergartners file into class, seating themselves at their tables in groups of four as they had been taught the first day of school. Not all of the lights in the classroom had been turned on. At the front of the class, the bank of bulbs near the large green chalkboard are still unlit. A bulb near the door flickers without rhythm, unable to turn completely on. The children sitting at the table under it laugh as they try to blink their eyes in time with its flickering. The children with tables nearest the chalkboard begin to wonder where the teacher is. Someone close to the coatroom shouts that it must be Saturday.

Within minutes the children seated beneath the flickering bulb begin to dance on top of their table. The shouting child near the coatroom swings from the flagpole mounted on the wall. Those nearest the chalkboard begin to cry. A few of the seated children remain relatively quiet as they gape at the classroom sights.

Though they do not sit at the same table, Molly and José's seats are quite close to one another since they are at adjoining tables.

"Don't say nothing," Molly tells José as she gets out of her seat. Taking a mat from one of the storage boxes under the window, she unfolds it in the area where the students normally take their afternoon nap, and lies down. With both arms wrapped around the red notebook, Molly closes her eyes and instantly begins to make quiet little snoring sounds. José unfolds a mat next to Molly and closes his eyes also. Soon the rest of the children are pulling out mats.

It is difficult to say how much time passes between the closing of the last pair of eyes and when Molly quietly sits up to examine the sleeping classroom. Walking quietly to Miss Conejo's desk, she sits down and opens the red notebook. She studies its pages intently, though she cannot read. After examining the notebook for nearly a minute, Molly closes it and removes a dictionary from the shelf next to the desk. This she sets on top of the closed notebook.

Leaving the teacher's desk, Molly walks around the classroom looking at each of the tables and then to the empty mat lying next to José. She folds up the mat, returns it to its storage box and then pushes open the classroom's playground door. Smiling to the sunlight, Molly skips away into the warm playground.

Some minutes pass and the classroom door opens. Molly pulls it as hard as she can and, before it closes all of the way, she pushes a flat of strawberries through the doorway. The closing door bumps into Molly from behind, pushing her back into the classroom. Once inside she picks up the flat, which is almost too large for her to carry, and walks the strawberries to the front of the classroom. Molly sets them on the floor just below the chalkboard.

Returning to the teacher's desk, Molly opens the dictionary and studies the small print inside. Flipping through several pages, she is unable to find any illustrations that might help her determine what story she has open before her. Closing the book, Molly examines its blank cloth cover and then notices a small embossed bird on the book's spine. As though this were enough, she reopens the volume. While moving her small fingers up and down the pages, she proceeds to recite out loud Hans Christian Andersen's story "The A-B-C Book" word-for-word from memory. At home, next to her bed, Molly has a small illustrated volume of such stories she sleeps with. As she recites this tale, the other children wake, put away the mats and return to their tables. There is snickering from somewhere near the coatroom as Molly recites the last line.

"Quiet!" Molly shouts, looking around the classroom attempting to locate the heckler. When her eyes come to José, she smiles and points to the strawberries on the floor.

"Excuse me, but who died and made you teacher?" asks a voice near the coatroom. Molly guesses this to be the heckler.

"*Nobody*, that's who's dying!" José shouts, jumping out of his chair.

"Let's have more story time!" says a child from José's table.

"First everybody gets a snack," Molly announces, walking toward the flat of strawberries. The children rush to the front of the room and quickly grab up the strawberries. A few try filling their pockets. Many of the smaller students return to their tables weeping and empty-handed. One child with two berries, shares with one of the empty-handed children.

Molly climbs onto the top of the teacher's desk and stamps her feet until everyone is looking at her. "Miss Conejo isn't here 'cause she crashed up her car."

José is suddenly wide-eyed. "She's just late! Her car didn't get smashed up!" he screams, jumping out of his seat again.

"She's not late. She got *killed* maybe," Molly adds, waving her arms in the air. José runs up to Molly and pulls her off the desk.

"You're gonna get me in trouble," José says, shaking her with tears in his eyes. "We wasn't supposed to go over there!" Molly knows that José is afraid of his father.

"Sit down or you'll have trouble for reals," Molly says pushing him back toward his table. The class has fallen silent and waits for José to sit down.

"Me and José was walking to school and Miss Conejo was driving very, very slow and she got crashed into by a another car. She was on the cherry street by the big church by our house and a sunlight from the church's big window made her not see the other car. She got smashed over and went upside down and . . . and she got squished with *blood*."

"It was by our house!" José shouts from his seat.

"She gave me her teacher book," Molly says, holding the red notebook over her head, "and told me I'm supposed to make sure everybody's in school. Don't tell nobody Miss Conejo gave me this, or she'll get some troubles. We'll all get big trouble."

"You said she might be dead," says the voice from the coatroom vicinity.

"She did got killed," Molly says, nodding her head.

The children nearest the chalkboard begin discussing how they already miss the teacher and wonder how they will continue school without her.

"We can all take turns being teacher!" yells a child, jumping up and down under the flag.

As the level of noise from discussion increases, the children beneath the flickering bulb climb back onto the table and resume their dance. Seeing this, the child jumping about under the flag runs to the light switches and pushes up the last one. The bulb near the door stops flickering as the final bank of bulbs at the front of the room lights up.

As the dancers return to their seats, the school bell rings. Some of the children begin to shout that it must be time for recess.

"We had a big nap time today," Molly announces, standing in front of the big green chalkboard, "so that's the bell that says it's time to go home."

This announcement is met with a loud hurrah and rush for the door. Within minutes the kindergarten yard empties as the children run and skip through the streetside gate.

In the kindergarten's playground there are two sandboxes. The smaller of the two is situated in the playground's far corner next to the chain link fence separating the kindergartners from the rest of the school. The large sandbox is perhaps twice its size and is located between the playhouse and jungle gym. This sandbox attracts many of the small children, while it is the smaller sandbox where the quiet children usually spend their recesses. Today, the day after Miss Conejo's accident, there are only two children in the small sandbox during recess; Craig and his brother Jeffrey.

Close to the small sandbox, in the main school yard, are the big kids' swings. The older children's morning break coincides with the kindergartners' only recess of their brief school day. Often, the children on the swings will make fun of the kindergartners closest to the fence, calling them such things as cry babies or monkeys in a zoo. Craig and Jeffrey rarely get upset by such name-calling. They continue to play, not allowing the older children's taunts to interfere with the construction of their most recent city. This morning; however, Nick, a child they know from their neighborhood, calls the two boys over to the fence.

"Hey Jeffy, my brother says you guys got no teacher in there," Nick says, poking a stick through the fence into the sand.

"Stop it, you're messing up our road!" Craig shouts, grabbing the stick out of the boy's hand.

"I ain't mess'n up nothin'!" he says, standing up. "So you monkeys got nobody to clean yer cage, huh?"

"Miss Conejo got killed by a car crash," Jeffrey says, as Craig pushes the stick back through to Nick's side of the fence, "so we get to be our own teachers now."

"You kids are full of it," Nick says, crossing his arms. "I saw Miss Conejo talkin' to Mr. Reynolds this morning."

Rather than respond to this last remark, the brothers return to their construction site in the sand. Craig imitates a combustion engine as he pushes a rusted yellow tractor through a pit that should soon be breaking through to China.

"You're stupid liars!" Nick says, throwing the stick at the fence. He stares at the boys for a moment and then runs off toward the other side of the playground.

Jeffrey watches Nick dash away and then disappear into a crowd of children. Once he is out of sight, Jeffrey borrows Craig's tractor to repair the damaged road bordering the fence.

The two boys become so involved with their system of roads and fancy gates that they do not hear the bell ring. They continue to play while all of the other children return to class.

In the school's main playground, a few of the more troublesome children often continue to play until they are certain that it is even time for the "pioneers," as they like to call themselves, to return to class. Today, the last of these "pioneers" are a couple of older boys on the swings. They do not sit quietly in an attempt to avoid being noticed, but swing wildly in high arcs that almost make them do midair flips. Finally, as the classroom doors begin to close, they leap from their swings and approach the fence next to the small sandbox. At first, neither of these two boys say a word as they study the handiwork of the two young brothers. Nearly a minute passes before the older of the two clears his throat in order to get Craig and Jeffrey's attention.

"Nice castle, guys, but you better get inside before your teacher catches you out here."

Jeffrey looks up from the sand and stares at the empty playground. Craig continues to make little rumbling noises as he pushes up more sand out of the growing pit.

"We won't get into trouble. Molly's teacher today," Jeffrey says turning his smiling face toward the two older boys.

"Oh yeah, somebody said you kids are alone in there," the older boy says. Jeffrey stands up to speak with the older boys.

"Who's Molly?" the older boy's companion asks.

"Molly sat at the white table," Craig says without looking up, "but she's in charge of us today."

The older boy motions Jeffrey to come closer. Looking secretively from side to side, he tilts his head forward as though to whisper. As Jeffrey leans against the fence, the older boy hooks a finger on the collar of his shirt.

"If you kids are lying," he whispers to Jeffrey, "Mr. Reynolds is gonna expel you or somethin'."

Standing up, Craig brushes the sand off his hands and runs off toward the kindergarten classroom as the older boy holds Jeffrey against the fence. A few moments later, Craig reappears followed by Molly, who is carrying the red notebook.

"Let go a him," Molly says nearing the fence. "He's missing story time."

"Oh yeah?" the older boys says releasing Jeffrey. "He says you kids got no teacher in there."

"No, I'm teacher today," Molly says, leaning into the fence next to the older boy. She sticks out her tongue and then adds sharply "Jeffy gets to be teacher *next* time."

"Do you kids know what kind of trouble you're gonna get when Miss Conejo finds out you're out here after recess?" the older boy says giving Molly a light push. Molly opens the notebook and pulls out a pencil from its cover pocket.

"What's your guys' names?" she asks with the pencil poised, ready to take notes.

"I'm Tommy and he's Matt," the older boy says, trying to peer into Molly's notebook. "Whatcha doin'?"

"Writing your names in the book," Molly says, smiling, "'cause you're being bad."

"No way!" Tommy says, "Let's see."

Molly tilts the notebook so Tommy can take a look. Although her attempt at writing his name was not very good, he observes the notebook indeed contains much of the same paperwork as his own teacher's notebook.

"Today's Friday," he comments, examining the blank role sheet. "You guys are gonna get caught with that blank paper."

"No we're not," Molly says, smiling, "Craig took the tendance paper to the office lady this morning. My sister Lisa told me she'll tell me when it's Fridays."

"You kids are somethin'," Tommy says. "If you guys have no real teacher, the principal's gonna make you go home."

"We been our own teacher for a long time," Jeffrey says.

"Oh yeah?" Tommy says, eyeing the notebook, "Then let me see you guys make the principal do somethin' right now."

"Like what?" Jeffrey asks.

"Ask Mr. Reynolds to give you a movie to watch."

"Oh," Molly says, flipping through the papers in the notebook, "which paper is that?"

Matt pokes his finger through the fence "I think it's that one," he says, pointing to a small yellow slip.

"I don't know any movies," Molly says, looking at the slip.

"I do," Tommy says, holding out his hand. "Gimme the pencil."

Molly passes Tommy a yellow slip and the pencil. After filling out the top part of the slip, he pushes it back through the fence along with the pencil.

"All you gotta do now's sign it!" he laughs.

Molly looks at the slip for a moment before writing her name on its backside in large crooked letters. She hands the slip to Craig, who immediately dashes off toward the school's office. "Let's go Jeffy," Molly says, turning around.

"Wait a minute," Tommy says, "we want to see if this is for real."

"Jeffy, go tell José to read everybody a numbers book. I'll wait for the movie."

After Jeffrey leaves, Molly seats herself on the edge of the sandbox. She stares at Tommy and Matt, who have already begun to survey the main school yard for roaming adults. After a few minutes, they begin to fidget considerably.

"We gotta get going," Tommy says, looking over his shoulder. "The kid's probably hiding out in the bathrooms or somethin'."

"Look!" Matt says, staring in the direction of the office.

Grinning from ear to ear, Craig enters the kindergarten's interior gate waving over his head what is obviously a movie.

"Next time," Molly says, standing up. "Craig's maybe gonna take a note on you guys."

Tommy and Matt step away from the fence as Molly holds the red notebook in front of her to punctuate her threat. The two boys offer Molly their friendliest smiles, then wave to Craig before running off to their classrooms.

△

It is uncertain exactly how many of the school's classrooms have teachers the following spring. There have been mixed reports from the school's office. Officially, Mr. Reynolds, the school's principal, refuses to comment, while his secretary has unofficially stated that the school seems to be running better than ever. In town, there is a rumor that not a single teacher returned after winter break.

On the Friday before spring break, there is a fight between a few of the older children. This scuffle breaks out between the swings and the kindergarten playground. It is only after several noses are bloodied that Mr. Reynolds arrives to escort the injured to the nurse's office. After the crowd breaks up, Tommy tells some of the kindergartners in the small sandbox that the children taken to the nurse's office were fighting over the now controversial subject of Miss Conejo. It is almost certain that Mr. Reynolds is going to investigate.

Tommy barely finishes this warning when Mr. Reynolds appears at the interior kindergarten gate. Most of the small children hide in the playhouse while a few merely cover their eyes in terror.

Without taking notice of the half hidden children, Mr. Reynolds walks directly into the classroom. A few moments later, he reappears with the red notebook tucked under his arm and heads back to his office. Just inside of the interior gate he stops for a moment and then turns around smiling.

"Children, your attention please," he announces loudly. "The school year's nearly over. You've all been very good, and so I hope you all enjoy a well-deserved spring vacation."

Understanding this to be a dismissal for the day, the children cheer wildly as they rush about collecting their belongings before going home.

Standing beside the classroom door, Molly cries quietly.

The Dirt Farmer

I find that it is impossible to work in my garden, or even pass by it, without remembering some bit of its history. The many stories which belong to each flower and rock that have come and gone. Often when I work in it, I think of how I came to live in this house in the desert.

Between a narrow concrete walkway connecting the front door of the house to the driveway and the stucco wall of a two-car garage lies a long and narrow patch of soil. "Soil" is a word which has a connotation of richness. This is far from what the soil, or perhaps more simply dirt, was when this house was new. The ground here, in this part of Apple Valley, consists mostly of clay and little else. Clay by itself is probably the worst possible soil in which to attempt to grow anything. The developer of this tract apparently was aware of this fact and thought this long, narrow patch of clay would benefit from the addition of unused plaster, scrap lumber and concrete. This unique composition has proved incapable of sustaining any plant life other than the weeds and wildflowers which are indigenous to this area. Over the years, I have removed the waste building materials and have worked the soil so that it has become rich. I am very fond of my garden. I do not have to look at it hard to see the years of my life that I have spent in it.

The roots of this garden are far older than this house. They reach beyond this concrete walk and stretch beyond this street. These roots are deepest here, in the desert, yet they stretch far beyond this place. Some of their furthest tips touch a small home some hundreds of miles away.

It was a little more than ten years ago when I left an excellent job with no future and moved from a small Northern California town to

Houston with my wife, Judy. Like many other people during that time, we were following opportunity.

I remember the day we left our Pleasanton home quite well. Knuckles were bruised on doorjams as we emptied the furniture from our home. Boxes upon boxes of belongings were stuffed into a too-small U-Haul truck. Just as we were about to drive away, I ran back to the house. We had almost forgotten a small clay pot which sat next to the sliding glass door on the back porch. To this day, I cannot remember what grew in that small pot. Possibly some small flower which had long since dried up and blown away. This small pot held soil from our yard.

Life in the Houston area was rather bizarre. We lived just outside of the small town of Tomball, and so conducted much of our personal business there. This small town was slow paced and appeared to be stuck in the year 1953. Pickup trucks sporting gun racks and Confederate flags were one of the more popular forms of transportation with the local gentry. South Texas was a world we had never expected. After three months of life in a part of Texas which had declared itself a nation, we decided it would be best to return to California. Because of the situation which we found ourselves in, we left Houston with little more than our clothes and sanity. Something we did not leave behind, however, was that little pot of soil.

Judy and I landed in Apple Valley. It was there that my sister, her husband and four daughters had recently bought a home on an acre of land. Fortunately for Judy and I, this gave us a place to stay until we could gain control of our lives again. It was not too long before I found a decent job and we moved into a small apartment. It was in August, two months after we moved, that we promised each other that living here, in the desert, was only temporary. We had to return to Northern California soon. The hot, dry air and sand were more than we could deal with. We could not imagine living here and remaining in our right minds.

A year later our son was born. We still lived in the same small apartment, and Judy had planted some daisy seeds in a small clay pot she found in the back of our storage cabinet. Our life before coming here was quickly becoming distant memories.

After a couple of prosperous years, we decided that it was time to consider buying a home. We knew this recently widowed woman, Ellen Magnuson, who had decided to either rent or sell her home. We agreed to rent this house with the intent of purchasing it in the near future.

The house was located in an older neighborhood. The street it was on was charming, with older yards and immense thirty-year-old liquid amber trees. Our backyard had a wonderful lawn and a huge fruitless mulberry. In a corner of the yard was an old vegetable garden that had belonged to Ellen's husband.

After her husband's death, Ellen refused to water the garden, and it soon died, too. One of the first things I did after we moved was to empty that small clay pot of dirt into one corner of the garden. The garden's soil was already incredibly rich and profited little by the addition of this new soil.

One Saturday afternoon I was rummaging around in the garage. It seemed obvious that the last person to seriously rummage about in there was Ellen's dead husband. Ellen had moved out and had not bothered get rid of the junk which prevented the garage from serving its intended function. Mr. Magnuson had a large workbench along the side of the garage. The bench had lots of wonderful little drawers and shelves with cupboard doors and had the appearance of being custom made. Upon close examination, I discovered that no two doors or handles were alike. No two screws either, as far as I could gather.

Beneath the top of the work bench, I discovered a large cardboard box filled with capped mason jars. I pulled out a jar which was filled with dried leaves. On the jar was a gummed label with faded ink. I imagined the faded ink had been intended to identify the jar's contents. Walking out the garage's side door, I held the jar to the sun and guessed bay leaves. No, more likely they were eucalyptus leaves. The markings on another jar were not nearly as faded—*Nettle*. The next jar contained lily, another mistletoe. Six more jars and the box was nearly empty. The glass of the last jar was light green. Instead of a gummed label, this jar had a paper tag attached to the end of a short string that was tied to the lid's wire clamp—*For the gold-haired man, Periwinkle.* The tag was signed, *Alberto.* I gave the jar a little shake and then popped open the top. The bit of plant inside did not seem entirely dry yet. I wondered if it had been meant to be kept green or if it somehow needed to be dried out. As I closed the jar's lid, I noticed more writing on the tag's back side—*Big worms in garden.*

In one of the work bench drawers I discovered some sweet pea seeds that had never been planted. Though it was too late in the year I made tiny little furrows in the soil I had recently turned. After a week or so, the seeds sprouted. There was a small fence around the garden, and from the back porch it was difficult to notice the little plants. I never mentioned the peas, so I doubt anyone ever noticed there was life in the garden. It seemed that the peas were a secret between Mr. Magnuson and myself. The seeds had been planted very late, and within a few weeks it was autumn. The sweet peas died shortly after flowering.

By the following spring, my wife and I discovered that the thirty-year-old home we were in had thirty-year-old house problems. The neighborhood was beautiful, the house charming; but between broken pipes and leaking faucets, we decided it would be to our best interest to purchase a new home that would have only new-house problems. After two months of searching, we bought a new home. A month later we began to move.

After little consideration, we decided that moving across town just didn't warrant renting a large truck, or even a trailer. We would just sort of shuttle carloads of boxes and loose belongings. When it got down to the piano, sofa, and so forth, well, we would call friends with trucks. That was a mistake not to be repeated. Our move across town took a great deal more time and effort than moving across the country.

It took us a week to move completely. The day after we had completely emptied the old house, I returned to its garden with a spade and a large cardboard box. I filled the box completely with soil from the garden where the peas had grown. After the box was filled to the top I discovered it could not be moved. I emptied most of the soil from the box and then put the box into the trunk of my car. I made several trips from the backyard to the car with a coffee can I retrieved from the trash. I felt a bit foolish when I noticed that our nosey former neighbor from across the street was scrutinizing me with some interest. I am sure it only took about a dozen trips back and forth to refill the box, but under the old guy's watchful stare, it seemed like it took hours to carry off the only decent soil in town. Having finished, I waved and smiled widely as I started the car's engine. With satisfaction, I observed that my waving sent the old guy indoors.

With the help of an old red wagon, the box of dirt ultimately ended up in the garage near the washer, and after a couple of days, Judy began to ask questions.

"What's with the dirt?"

I did not have a reply which could make sense, not to her, so I am sure the whole thing seemed a bit foolish. After the box sat on the garage floor for a couple of weeks, it seemed as though she had stopped thinking about it. At that time, I still had not decided upon a fitting use for the soil. I began to think about the strip of dirt which followed along the front walk to the door. It would make a wonderful flower garden.

One afternoon, perhaps a week after I began to think of starting a flower garden, I came home to find Judy sitting cross-legged on the front walk in tears.

"I've been out here all afternoon trying to plant these daisies. I might as well try to plant them in the driveway."

On the walk next to her was a small "six-pack" of plants. The four holes she had finished were only a couple of inches deep and apparently had cost her a blister each. I looked into each of the little holes.

"Dirt won't take water anyway." I said, thinking out loud.

Judy just sat there staring into the dirt with tears running down her cheeks. Suddenly, she looked up, smiling.

"That dirt, the dirt in the garage . . ." She was rather excited, "It's to fix the yard, isn't it? Bring it out and mix it in. Tonight—please?"

"Ah . . . well . . ." Now I was the one staring into the dirt. I knew she would not want to hear that the large box of dirt would only be enough soil for one medium-sized plant and not much more. Braving the prospect of more tears, I did explain. With that, we decided to make a trip to the hardware store.

We returned home with a small rosebush, several bags of planting mix and mulch. The rose was full of leaves, but without any buds. There was no tag in its branches, like the other plants, only a price sticker affixed to its bucket. Of course, we knew it was a rose, but of what sort—that was going to be a surprise.

I spent half of the following Saturday digging the hole in which the rose was going to be placed. Late in the afternoon, I emptied most of the soil from the box in the garage around and underneath the rosebush. The remainder of the soil I literally sprinkled about the garden as though it were pixie dust. As I did this, I knew that so little could not possibly help this water-resistant clay. Perhaps with some time and labor on my part, I could help to fake a miracle.

I have never been fond of the sort of flower gardens that are arranged in color-coordinated neat little rows. Pansies here, flanked by sharp rows of yellow marigolds. Such a garden seems a bit like something one would see at an amusement park. Something like a military parade in miniature.

I have always admired the sort of gardens you see in those fake Romantic paintings. The sort of pictures that depict quaint little cottages in the English countryside. The gardens generally shown are the sort where the flowers appear to have been cast about like stones in a fanning pattern. As it happens, that is just how that sort of garden is laid out. The gardener will cast a number of stones and plant certain flowers where the stones fall. Like so. Though we were a bit limited by space, this is the sort of chaos Judy and I wanted.

With the exception of the various rosebushes which have been planted over the years, all of the flowers and plants came from bulbs or seeds. As difficult as it might seem, we came to know every plant in the garden intimately. Generally, it was known which plants were about to flower and with how many blooms. Quite often, an opening bud would fetch everyone outside to admire its beauty. The garden became filled with a wild variety of color. English daisies here, cinnamon-scented carnations there. On the side of the bed which bordered the garage wall, a tall border of iris, lilies and roses were all mixed together. Between all of these flowers, the soil of the bed became densely hidden under a covering of clover and alyssum.

During summer evenings, I enjoyed carefully handwatering the entire garden. While watering, I would admire all of the flowers and would keep an eye open for intruding weeds. Often while collecting small seeds or moving bulbs about, I would be freed, briefly, from those things which troubled me. For me, the garden was an escape and a marvelous place for quiet thought. I have often given, or rather lost, much of myself there.

That first rosebush, the one without tags, had become a beautiful large, red rosebush. Its fragrance was strong and wonderful. This bush created the most beautiful roses I have ever known. It was as though all of my care and reflections in the garden were being manifested in the flowers of this one bush. And so, often when there would be a particularly beautiful rosebud just about to open, I would watch it carefully for a day or so. Then, at the perfect moment, I would snip off the rose. This rose I would give to Judy. After the first couple of years in the new house, I began to notice something rather odd. I began to observe that the rosebuds would sometimes disappear, often just before they were perfect. These roses never materialized in water-filled vases around the house. Although I had a fair notion, I never asked where they disappeared to.

It was at this time that Judy and I began to plant stones in the garden. These were generally retrieved from meaningful places such as Lake Arrowhead, where we both lived for many years, or more frequently from places Judy and a friend visited around the valley. These stones would be arranged into borders, or would be piled into the thick of clover.

I remember once "borrowing" a large granite boulder from Mt. Gregory. This rock appeared as though it had been painted all over in black and yellow. Actually this "paint" was thick patches of lichen. The black and yellow contrasted nicely, making the stone rather handsome. After a couple of months, the regular watering and shade seemed to kill the lichen. I think now that it may have been the rocks and stones Judy and I planted that eventually killed the garden.

Today, only I tend this garden of stones. I have long stopped watering. The loss of the roses really does not bother me very much, I no longer have anyone to give them to. It was rather surprising to see how quickly all the plants died and the soil returned to clay. Perhaps I should take a spade and turn it all over . . .

One Way Donkey Ride

There once was a rather ordinary young man who lived in a small town. One bright spring morning, many years ago, this young man woke suddenly to the singing of a little robin outside of an open bedroom window. The young man's eyes opened in shock at the realization that he was in a bed he could not recall climbing into the night before.

The young man leapt from under the covers onto the cold bare floor. Dazed by the sunlight, the young man gazed about at the unfamiliar sight of a comfortably decorated bedroom. After a few moments, he noted that a jingling noise was coming from his pajamas pocket. Reaching deep inside his pocket, he felt for whatever it was that could be tinkling there. He removed his hand and beheld a tiny golden key. How odd, but stranger still was this unfamiliar room. Whose house was this anyway? His eyes fell to the bed and the mess of its sheets. How embarrassing. Should he attempt to tidy up? Or should he just beat a retreat before being found out?

Dressing rather quickly and haphazardly, the young man roamed about the house in hope of locating the front door. He could not help but notice how delightfully the various rooms of this house were decorated. After a few moments, he found himself out-of-doors and on the front porch breathing in the crisp morning air. The front door swung closed behind him, making a soft click. As it did so, the young man stopped for a moment. At first he looked toward the pretty yard and an attractive flower garden. Collecting himself, he decided that it might be best to move along.

Just as he was about to step off the porch, he glanced back to the door. It is often impetuous or thoughtless acts such as this which set fate into motion. Were it not for this momentary backward glance, this young man would never have seen the tiny keyhole above the knob. He dug the tiny golden key from his pocket.

The tiny golden key and lock were a set. Upon the door, only slightly higher than eye level, he saw a brass knocker. On it, his surname was engraved in fancy script letters. Now things were becoming a bit peculiar. Without bothering to lock the door behind him, the young man pocketed the tiny golden key and wandered off into the garden.

After several years of a comfortable life with this pretty little house, the young man found himself frightened late one afternoon as he discovered that the pretty little house was jolting about uncontrollably. It was as though a tremendous earthquake were about to knock the pretty little house off its foundation.

Outside, workmen in dungarees and t-shirts were busy lifting the pretty little house off its foundation and onto the bed of an oversized tractor-trailer. A foreman handed the confused young man an envelope. Inside were a few papers. Papers with tiny little print. Papers explaining how the young man's lease had lapsed and the pretty little house was being moved to a new location, possibly to be put up for sale at some later date. Soon the workmen had the pretty little house uprooted. As he watched the pretty little house disappear, the young man dug the golden key from his pocket and dropped it to the cold ground. The young man walked off, with the sunset at his back.

As he slowly walked along the road, he noticed that there were houses on all sides. Many had flower gardens out front and freshly mowed lawns. Many of the houses were very pleasant looking, though occasionally he would pass by one that had not been kept up very well at all. One thing he did notice was that, for the most part, all of these houses appeared to be lived in. Each one seemed to have its occupant. After a while, this began to bother the young man. He ceased admiring the lovely gardens and began to scrutinize the inhabitants of the houses. Occasionally, one of these houses would have a sign out on its front lawn which would read something like "ROOM FOR RENT." A rented room was not a very appealing thought to the young man. Imagine, renting a room from somebody he hardly knew. He was accustomed to living in his own house. No matter. These houses, regardless of how attractive they seemed, just were not right anyway. Each one of them had lacked that "special something."

As the long shadows surrounding the young man grew longer and darkness closed in, it occurred to him that he had no place to sleep for the night. Walking perhaps another mile or so, he stopped beneath a large tree. It was here that he lay down and fell fast asleep.

In the morning, the young man awoke to the caw of a raven perched atop a nearby telephone pole. Not far away, a huge billboard was planted squarely in the middle of a yard. In large red letters this billboard announced "HOUSE FOR SALE." In much smaller letters, and all in one corner, were instructions to direct *all* inquiries to a local realtor. The young man peered around the billboard and noticed that the house behind it was very bright and attractive. The garden was a virtual rainbow of color. Looking toward the opposite end of the bright house, he observed through the kitchen window a middle-aged man having his morning coffee. Perhaps it would be appropriate to introduce himself to the occupant. Maybe make an offer on the bright house, thereby cutting out the expense of any third party. The young man approached the front door and thought long about giving it a good loud bang. As the young man was about to do just that, the door flung open and the middle-aged fellow from inside popped out.

The two men stood on the front steps of the bright house and exchanged a few sharp words. The middle-aged man, with great irritation, explained that *his* bright house was, in fact, *not* for sale. The young man demanded an explanation as to what the intent of the huge billboard was. The middle-aged fellow merely waved him off and exclaimed that the bright house was definitely not for sale.

The young man eventually wandered into the business district of this little town. As it happened, the bright house was, in fact, for sale. The middle-aged man, who fancied himself its owner, just had not been aware of that fact yet. The bright house was very expensive. It would cost much more than the young man had ever imagined spending, but the young man judged that it would be worth it. He was tired of looking for a house, and this one had seemed awfully bright and attractive.

Later that afternoon, the young man decided that he may as well move into the bright house. Quietly making his way up the front walk, he examined the immense billboard which was planted in the front lawn. That billboard would have to go first thing in the morning. That might prove to be a difficult task, however; its posts were not just driven into the lawn, they actually appeared to have been cemented into place.

Entering the front door, the young man bumped into the middle-aged man, who was just leaving. Without looking up, the middle-aged man handed over a great set of bright brass keys and a large pink plastic fob which hung on a short length of baling wire.

"Good luck," the middle-aged man muttered, and then stumbled down the walk toward the street. It was the end of a very long day for the young man, so he went straight to bed.

In the morning, he thought that it would be nice to wander about the bright house and become acquainted with it. He soon discovered that the bright house consisted of little more than a small bedroom and a kitchen. That was very aggravating. The young man had paid a great deal of money for what he had imagined would be a complete house; only now to discover that this bright house was nothing more than a bedroom with a porch. Upon further investigation, he found that the colorful skirt surrounding the foundation was just aluminum siding, the bright trim bordering the windows and front door were nothing more than cheap plastic molding, and as for the flowers in the garden, each one was some grotesquely oversized plastic thing which had been carelessly stuck into the shallow soil.

In a rage, the young man dashed indoors hoping to telephone the realtor and complain, but alas, there was no telephone either. Well, perhaps after a quick cup of tea he would walk back into town and complain in person. To the horror of the young man, he soon discovered that not only did the appliances fail to function, but the fuse box was missing completely. Enough was enough.

Upon the young man's arrival at the realtor's office, he discovered that a set of paperwork had already been prepared, transferring the bright house to a semi-professional ball team from Peoria. There was no need to leave the keys, a duplicate set had already been made. The young man suddenly and unexpectedly found himself without a house.

It certainly seemed to the young man that he was living in strange times, what with houses driving off into the sunset or suddenly changing hands apparently without the knowledge of the would-be owners.

Was it all so terrible, really? The young man no longer cared if he had a house or not. Why, just think of all that maintenance and yard work. He had only needed a place to sleep. Nobody ever said he had to buy. The young man really did not need a house, either; he could sleep out-of-doors in a tent if he had to. Why, houses were nothing but a load of work. The only reason he bought the bright house was because he was tired of always looking. He was tired of wandering along the road staring at all of those other houses.

The young man resigned himself to the life of a vagabond. He could live anywhere, sleep anywhere. He could even sleep over in someone else's house if he had to. So long as he never had to buy another house again. However, the image of wandering about alone on the road was not a very appealing one.

The young man was so convinced that he would never own a house again, that he stopped looking to see if there were "FOR SALE" signs out or not. The young man never stopped admiring the houses themselves though.

After a few years, a visitor friend of the young man's asked him why he did not consider buying a house so he could have a warm bed at the end of a long day. The young man considered disputing his visitor friend's question. What made his visitor friend think that a house would be a nice place to go to at the end of a long day? It then occurred to the young man that he would have been wrong to say such a ridiculous thing. How could he ever have imagined that a tent pitched along the roadside was as nice as a house?

The young man was surprised to find himself occasionally gazing through listings of houses for sale over his morning tea. He began to wander about unfamiliar neighborhoods admiring large beautiful yards.

The funny thing was, as much as the young man looked, he never saw a house which caught his fancy. Sometimes he would stumble upon a house that seemed attractive enough from the outside, but would soon discover that inside, it was completely full of bad wiring.

As time passed, the young man decided that he would just go on living in a tent. The perfect house, at least as he imagined it, obviously had not been built. He had seen so very many houses that he was now quite certain that he would recognize this home immediately, if he were ever to lay eyes on it.

Entirely by chance, for he had long since stopped looking, the young man spotted a house one evening. This house, which had caught his eye was down toward the end of a road he seldom traveled. He did not immediately investigate this house, but decided that he would return to look it over in the next day or so.

Well, it was a week or two later when the young man finally decided to have a closer look a this attractive little house. From the street, it seemed cozy. A wrought iron fence and gate kept out the unwelcome, but the garden and yard seemed warm enough. At one end of the yard, under a handsome shade tree, was a swing set. The young man looked about. The gate was locked and there was no sign indicating the house was for sale. It seemed unlikely that it would be, either. This house was quite obviously inhabited. The young man went home to his tent thinking of this attractive little house.

The following week, the young man stopped by this same little house again, hoping that nobody would be too curious as to what he was doing as he strolled around the periphery of the wrought iron fence examining the wonderfully attractive house from all sides. It had a comfortable look to it. He squinted from the fence as he studied the trim surrounding the windows and doors. No plastic here, that was for sure. Wherever the curtains were drawn aside, he would try to peer indoors, hoping to get a glimpse of what the insides of this wonderful little house must look like. It was difficult to say. Why, he was not even sure if anyone was inside.

Again the following week, the young man stopped by that wonderful little house. As he came down the street, he could see that someone had left the front gate standing open. This was his opportunity to get a good, close look. With sweaty hands and heart pounding, the young man crept up to a window and peered inside. The curtains were drawn open. Pressing his nose to the glass, the young man looked into a large kitchen.

In the middle of this kitchen sat a large wooden table. On this table sat a cup and saucer. Next to these an open book, pages downward, a place being kept. The young man could see on the opposite side of the table an open door which led out of the kitchen. This door opened into some room, the nature of which the young man could not determine. What were those in the other room? Books? They were indeed books, and the shelves they were on appeared as though they may have been built directly into the wall itself. Maybe even connected to the frame of the house itself! Interesting. It is rare to find a house constructed so well. On the wall next to the shelves . . . was that a color sketch of some long ago Canadian Indian? The young man's gaze returned to the interior of the kitchen. On the wall, above a vase of pink roses sitting upon the buffet next to the door, hung a pair of beautiful blue china dishes.

The young man recognized the Wedgewood pattern. It is here that he was caught. Caught staring into a pair of sky blue saucers suspended above a couple of roses. Unseen, but from somewhere within, a soft hushed voice asked the young man if he saw anything of interest. Slowly, the young man lowered his gaze so as not to shatter the saucers. Slowly so that . . . so that *nothing* shattered. And then, without bothering to rush (for he had already been caught), the young man slowly walked down the long drive. Just as he was about to step off of the drive and into the lane, the young man heard from a distance in the yard behind him the abrupt rustling of wings, and then a faint sound which he could only barely hear. Without looking back, the young man strode onto the lane and away from the beautiful little house.

Later, as the young man sits in his tent, his visitor friend stops by for a few minutes.

No, the young man will not be looking at any more houses.

Why not? The visitor friend is curious.

No reason; well, none really. The young man explains to his visitor friend that he has already found his dream house. Problem is, someone is already living in it. It is entirely unlikely that the beautiful house will ever be vacated.

The visiting friend is confused by this response. Why should the young man not continue to look?

The young man attempts to explain. He cannot continue to search for what he has already found. It would be pointless.

The visitor friend looks at the young man for a moment. What seems to be the problem here? After all, a house is a house.

The young man tells his visitor friend how he was able to briefly peek into an open window of this amazing house. He tries to explain what he had seen there.

What sort of craziness is this? One open window and the young man is resolved to live as a tramp? The visitor friend is now very much bewildered.

After a few moments of silence, the young man chokes back what may have been a laugh. He then proceeds to point out the excellent quality and features of his newest tent.

Morning Glory

Crawling along, stop and go, on the I-10 through downtown Los Angeles, my head began to spin—my vision became confused. I thought I might black out; slam on the gas instead of the brake and jump off the freeway toward who knows what. I held on tightly to the steering wheel—staring straight ahead. My heartbeat was in my ears. For some reason, I was sure my time was up. Maybe it was an aneurism. I thought of the dinner party Saturday night, and how I had drunk too much. Always too much. Well, too much lately anyway. Perhaps I should slow down a bit. After all, my father died from cirrhosis of the liver. No, I just should have eaten something before leaving this morning. *Quack-quack.*

I have always been wise enough to know when to pull off the freeway and give it a break. I know I must have saved my mother more grief than she deserved on many occasions by pulling over and sleeping it off. I mean as a teenager—you know, coming home late and such.

At something like Temple or First, I thought I might try to find something to eat.

At an intersection, a homeless fellow was flirting with women drivers waiting for the light to change. He operated a clever cardboard sign with flaps which said different things. He flipped them about wildly. *Please Help* disappeared and a smiling face appeared. Another flip, and *Beautiful Woman* appeared. He straightened up with a smile. The women laughed, but windows remained up. When the signal turned green, he flipped the sign over. It said *God Bless You*, but I'm sure that message was intended only for the redhead in the next lane.

I could have been in Little Tokyo, I suppose, except when I stopped, it was fish tacos, not sushi for lunch. So I must have been somewhere else. I thought I was supposed to pick up my brother, Steve, at the train station, but then remembered he had died recently. Vietnam? No, it was Dave who died in Vietnam. Steve, on the other hand, he was in Chino or Chico, or some such place. I guess I was supposed to pick him up next week.

Later, I pulled into a gas station, where I tried to call my boss to let him know I had trouble with my car. I asked if he could have a tow truck meet me in Glendale, maybe in an hour or so. I know he doesn't like people calling him at home, but sometimes you just have to.

The gas station had a small, dirty office with a desk and no restroom. The cash register was mounted on a pole next to the pump. Next to a broken down car and the street entrance to the station was an open hole with what appeared to be a manhole cover next to it. It was much larger than those holes they drop a stick into to measure how much gas is left.

"Be careful not to fall into the open sewer," the attendant said, as I approached the hole. "Maintenance people are having problems with stuff down there." Next to the cover was a pile of what looked like a coiled orange garden hose. One end disappeared into the open hole. There was water sloshing out of the top of the hole onto the ground, and so I guessed the hose must be some sort of breathing apparatus. Like those guys in diving suits who explore the bottom of the ocean. I looked around for a truck or some sort of pump. Something the free end of the hose should be connected to. I looked at the attendant thinking he might know where the other end should go. I mean, men have to breathe, right? Well, he said not to worry. The maintenance men were off at lunch and took all the pumps and stuff with them.

It was a good thing I took a second look at that hose before heading back to my car. The end that was stuck into the hole was beginning to disappear slowly. Kind of like somebody was at the other end trying to make off with it quietly so as not to be noticed; or, I thought, more likely a fish—getting ready to take off with the goods.

I waved at the attendant to come take a look. As soon as he saw that hose slipping away, he let out a "hey!" He said I should stop before I got in trouble or something. I said that it wasn't my fault and grabbed onto the hose. The attendant said he knew I didn't mean anything by it, and that he would go get his boss.

Well, let me tell you, pulling that hose back out wasn't nearly so easy as standing there watching it disappear. At first, I coiled up what came out of the hole onto the pile. I couldn't stand it though. It wasn't just water in there. The hose came out covered with all sorts of muck. At one point, something strange and white slipped off the hose and fell to the asphalt with a wet plop. It didn't take long before I could feel there was something large and heavy down below somewhere.

Pulling the hose from the sewer quickly became difficult work. The coils next to the hole were growing high and if I were to let go, the entire line was certain to disappear. Suddenly I found that I was handling a heavy chain. Perhaps this was the heavy weight. The hose was attached to the chain with a thin rag which lashed the two ends together in much the same way a farmer might lash two poles together. This joint just fell apart when I placed my foot on it though. I was amazed it held together as long as it did.

I didn't want to let go of the chain and let it just go whizzing back into the water. I'm sure *somebody* didn't want it getting away. I didn't get far, thinking I could just hook one end of the chain onto the first thing around, when I realized this chain was actually quite short. I hadn't pulled the chain halfway back to the gas pump when I saw something green being dragged up out of the hole. The owner of the station ran out of the office and held the end of the chain while I went to examine what was coming up. The chain had obviously broken, and somebody had spliced in a bit of morning glory vine in order to keep it intact. A good thing, too, because the load was becoming more than I could bear, and it was quickly becoming a two-man job to haul out whatever was down there.

We pulled that second piece of chain over to the station owner's pickup truck and wrapped a couple of loops around its trailer hitch. As soon as he got in the cab and gave it the gas, wheels spun and the air filled with the stink of hot rubber and smoke. The truck was quickly losing ground. Whatever was down there was going to take down the truck with it, so I pulled off the chain before it was too late.

After I managed to inch the chain a few more feet out of the hole, a strange form suddenly bobbed to the surface. It took a moment before I realized the brown rusted mass coming up was one end of what appeared to be a huge iron billet. What the end the chain was welded onto could easily have been a foot and a half square. I imagined it must have been nearly as long a freight car. After a few more heaves, I decided I would never be able to get that thing out on my own. I let go of the chain and let the entire show snake off back into the sewer. As it was, I figured somebody was lucky I had saved the hose.

But it's not like that. I thought of my how my father always had one eye open to find out who was responsible. It never really mattered who it was—anyone would do. Sometimes my brother Dave was guilty of nothing more than trying to make something right. Thinking of this, I slipped one end of the hose back into the hole so it just touched the water. I hurried back to my car because somewhere, most likely Glendale, a tow truck was waiting for me.

Why I Hate Pets

—for Russell Errett

I don't like thinking of it too much, but the truth is, one of us is insane. One of us is insane and needs to get out of the house.

I am thinking of my son, Jack, and the things he says sometimes. He talks to himself. He does this frequently, which is annoying since it makes it difficult for me to hear myself think. For instance—now this has nothing to do with his talking to himself, or at least very little—but for instance, last Sunday evening, I'm trying to read or write or do something, it doesn't really matter at this point, but I am sitting there sipping my margarita when *bam*! this black plastic ball rolls into the living room and smacks into the grandfather clock.

This gets my attention, since it's under the clock where my son's python, Lucy, has been hiding out lately and I don't want the little serpent to get upset again. I stare at the ball and it just sits there, completely immobile for a few seconds and then, apparently of its own accord, begins to roll toward the pantry. Halfway there, it changes direction suddenly and heads directly for my feet and then slows to a stop.

"What the . . ." I say, grabbing the ball for closer examination. I eye Jack, who at this point is fairly well self-involved in a bowl of cereal and jerking his head back and forth humming some Bob Dylan tune I could really care less about. Jack is responsible for the ball, I'm certain. If there's something odd in the house, it belongs to Jack. Indeed, to me the ball *is* odd.

"Yours?" I ask, holding the ball out.

"Sort of," says Jack. The fact that he can't answer a question is a bit annoying. Looking closely at the ball I can see right away that it's no wind-up toy.

"What kind of batteries does it take?" I ask.

"No batteries," he says. I think about this for a moment; *a plastic black ball is rolling about the living room on its own. It is neither electrical nor mechanical*. . . I tell Jack that I do not believe it's possible that there's no place for batteries. *Something* causes the ball to move. Jack laughs and says that it does not move on its own and the explanation is simple. He says he will reveal the secret of the ball to me if I promise not to tell anyone. He looks around secretively, and I have to admit he's got me kind of curious. He gives me a wink, indicating all's clear, I suppose, and then gives the ball a little twist and pulls it apart into two halves. In one half sits his pet gerbil, Dawkins.

"It's operated *biologically*," he says. I ask why he doesn't put the gerbil into one of those clear plastic balls so he can see where he is going. Jack says that it's much more fun to watch Dawkins run about the house when he has no idea of where he is going, and an opaque ball seemed more humane than the old needle in the eye thing, which he has never really cared for.

"Because it's a cruel thing to do, but kind of amusing?" I ask, meaning the opaque ball.

"No, because Dawkins is *God*," he says. It is at this point I hold my hand up, indicating he is going to need to hold onto that thought long enough for me to mix myself another margarita.

Now it seems to me that this claim that his pet gerbil is God seems fairly ridiculous. I've been doing a little reading this last week and I'm certain I'm tooled up and ready to surprise Mr. Know-It-All when he tries to say something about how the ball moved without another mover.

Note to self: *At this point I should have switched to coffee.*

"Okay," I say, grabbing the ball back, "I suppose this is where you go on about how the ball is being moved by something or someone else; and something about infinite progression or digression—and not being able to go off forever—and—and then there was nothing before something else and then there was something which was really hot or could have been hot because of—of—of . . ." I grab a book off the dining room table and start to search for the right page. I close one eye in order to focus; "because nothing can be reduced from potentiality to actuality, except by something in a state of actuality . . ." I read arrogantly.

"And what about this?" I ask pointing to some tiny writing molded into the inside of the ball. "It says right here, *Made in Indonesia*!" Jack stares at me for moment and says nothing. He assumes I'll keep going. I don't. Actually, what really surprises me is that I threw down that last margarita in two gulps.

"You've actually been reading that stuff?" he says pouring himself a glass of water. Jack only drinks *pure* distilled water. You should hear his theories on the bodily fluid thing.

"You bet," I say.

"What'd you think about that bit on efficient cause?"

"Made me dizzy," I admit.

Okay, at this point I give in. I concede. I ask Jack to explain the God comment. Was I even close to what he was thinking? "*Sort of*," he says. I ask him to come to the point. I tell him that I'm writing this all down and that I'd like to keep it to sixty-two books or less. Jack's a good kid, but the thing is, he thinks it's amusing to speak in parables. The fact is he just doesn't want to account for his own words later on.

Jack points to our pet turtles, Anton and Eve. Anton, the smaller of the two, likes to climb up on Eve's back and sit there for much of the day.

"That," he explains, "or something very similar to that, is where the Hindus concocted their idea of the cosmos."

"Have you been talking to Russell again?" I ask. Russell is our next door neighbor. "This sounds like his *Hindu-Vindu* crap, and why he finally moved out of New York City."

Jack pretends not to hear me. Russell has friends in low places and gets Jack his distilled water wholesale. Jack continues with his explanation about how the Hindu belief says that the world rests upon an elephant and this elephant rests upon a tortoise. *And where*, as he says Russell would ask, *does the tortoise rest*? Well, Jack explains, the Hindu analogy is exactly the opposite from reality. He believes that nearly everything around us rests on a tortoise and the tortoise rests on an elephant and the elephant rests on the earth. And the earth; it's a free floating ball in space. Now, like other heavenly bodies, the earth's mere existence acts upon all other heavenly bodies, but that is only a function of natural law. The earth itself is without support . . .

". . . or so it would seem," he says, looking about again secretively.

"And this proves that Dawkins is God?" I say, thinking *this* is the Illuminati moment I've been waiting for. I would have thought that Russell would say that this line of thinking proves there is no God.

"*It is proof*," he says, and goes on about how the fact is, he believes, that when his gerbil is in his ball, the world rests on him, and therefore, that makes him God. Jack admits he's not so sure about the business of the tortoise and the elephant though; but all in all, it's that simple. When push comes to shove, it is necessary to admit that the world rests on something, and this something Jack and his friends have given the name of Dawkins.

"Now, if I can just get enough people to repeat that, it'll be true," he says.

Prince of the Synagogue

Yerushalayim. A word, no, a thought which comes as stars reflect in a shallow puddle of water and illuminate mother's belly. Awareness of myself is shocking while this other thought seems only vulgar, perhaps impossible. The thought remains.

The large master sounds like a bird as he paces slowly about the grass knoll between the others and this place. The grass and thick plants are plentiful near the brown water hole. The others do not come, and so there is much to be eaten. Longer leaves have an unusual taste, which is not as pleasing as that of the simple grass. These leaves must be eaten because of this difference.

Bird song ends. Both masters mumble at one another for a moment. Close up, their voices are a strange barking which is startling. Gradually, they wander toward the others, who are now on the knoll which has been eaten. Mother bleats from somewhere near the other water. I hurry toward her voice in hopes of milk. The small master is a distraction that turns me aside. He leads me back to the brown water.

Again with bird sounds, the larger one comes near. With calming strokes and a pat, he ties a short cord. I am drawn along in the sunshine and a warm blue sky. Brown water disappears into the distance. Too quickly to be bitten, grass and twigs disappear beneath feet.

After many hot days of running about at the end of this short cord, master drags me through a river of almost clear water. All around there is much barking and bleating. There are nearly as many masters as there are mothers.

On the other side of the river, I am placed upon the back of a beast of burden. Grabbing a short length of cord around this beast's neck, master ceases his bird song and begins to bark wildly. A turmoil of peculiar bleating follows behind.

How many days I do not know. Traveling upon another's back to strange places is almost difficult. With wet eyes, master holds out an open hand to another and then spits as he lets something fall into the other's outstretched hand.

He hisses something into my ear and then lifts me from the beast's back. I am bound up and carried through the stone door.

Mon Dieu, the bastards have broken my nose. How could such a young thing become so bitter? "*Je ne scay point de complices. Ay, laisso, siou mouert.*" Accomplices would mean a conspiracy. *I* am not the one allied in this trial.

Lightning would work very well just about know. Right here, right between the eyes. Father Gaufridi, now is not the time to lose faith. A miracle, however, would be apropos. Even a small thunderhead would do. This is your chance. Burn all of these bastards at once. I preferred the rats.

"*Levez-vous*! *Parlez*!"

Why? If I go up once more bound like, this I am done with. If I remain here, he shall only kick in a rib and hoist me anyway. Take me now, please! Rats! Yes, yes, feed me to the hungry rats.

Madeliene is crying; "*Ne vous levez pas*!"

I do not understand how she could have come to this. Accusations of bewitchment and seduction? What lesson is to be gleaned from this? Refuse the young one's confession? In the future, I shall endeavor to assign penance which would make this all worth the effort. It is nearly impossible to believe that lies could have come so easily to such sweet lips. The malicious imp.

With the best intentions of working these knees and feet, I can do little else but lie here. Somehow my spirit has gone out of the effort. Michaëlis, some assistance, please? This party has turned sour. I know, a bit of broken skull might dry those pathetic pools of tears in the corner. Sister, do you like magic tricks? Pay close attention and you shall observe that my hands never leave my back. A bit of bird song learned long ago, a little flapping of my feet and we take flight . . .

"*Parlez!*"

"*Yo diriou, Messiés, non siou pas christian*; *si noun lou disiot, ay conegut Magdalens a la sinagogo, parce que la conession de deca.*" Certainly renouncement of faith is a bit dramatic, yet anything is worth trying in order to be cut loose.

Michaëlis leans over and whispers into the ear of the young girl, who is now quite inconsolable. The door is unbolted, and the two leave before the real work begins. Ollivier shoves a couple of large weights toward my feet to keep me company. A bit slower than a thunderstorm, perhaps, but things are certainly beginning to look up. Perhaps you have been listening. Ollivier smiles and then moves his jaw about in an odd sort of way. Guards laugh.

Although she is beautiful, he does not love her.

△

"So what do you think?" Truthfully, I could care what Angela thinks.

"What? You're asking me? You're gorgeous. No, a goddess. With a perm like that, you're a goddess. I'm telling you though, Brian's going to kill you."

"I doubt seriously he'll want to *kill* me."

"Ooooo," Angela reaches for her purse, "but if he *does* decide to kill you Mary, give me a call okay?"

"Sure." I'm not sure that would amount to anything. I guess Angela could care less also.

Angela's four-year-old has a longer attention span than she does. "Where are you guys going this weekend?"

"Sherman's Island."

Twice the medication—this was my doctor's solution to chronic headaches and nightmares. The man's hardly a psychologist, but at least the headaches have subsided. Things have been a little more tolerable with Brian, anyway. No drugs and he says I'm a total witch. Strangely for some reason, I would rather he simply came right out and said that I was a total bitch. It wouldn't bother me, except for the fact that he seems to only say it when I'm feeling like I really am in my right mind.

Saturday afternoon on Sherman's Island I wake suddenly. It occurs to me that he's trying it again.

"Get away from me."

"Honey?"

I glare at him as he backs away slowly. The bastard is rubbing his hands together, I swear. "*Don't you touch me*!" He's actually wringing his hands. The bastard's tried it again, I know he has.

"Honey, have you had your medicine today?"

"Don't look at me!" Christ, he can be irritating.

"Honey?"

"I said no, okay? Are you happy now?"

"I . . ."

"Give me a beer." It's absolutely incredible how stupid he can be at times. Mother put me through numerous inquisitions attempting to figure out why I ever married the man. Was it security? Hardly. The man's an idiot. Does everyone need a definable motivation for everything in their life? Even before we got married something about him bothered me. As though *I* let that slow me down from saying yes. I guess I was out to prove something. He's out to get me though, I know it. Honest to God, if I catch him with those filthy hands around my throat one more time, I'll put a match to one of his manuscripts. Then I can see how *he* likes it.

"You sound like a sailor."

"Just shut up and give me a beer." The idiot digs about in his pocket and then holds out his keys.

"What do you say you take a drive over and pick up a case?"

"We're on an island, stupid." I say.

"Take the boat. You'll still need these." He jingles the keys in front of my face as though I don't have a brain in my head.

"Wallet." I should just leave him here and go home. Maybe then he'd learn to keep his hands to himself.

"Here." He holds out a twenty.

"Are you deaf? Give me your wallet." Maybe he's right; I might be a little off kilter. I'm sure I could find an open pharmacy in Pittsburgh. Shrugging, he stuffs the twenty back into the wallet and hands it over. He clears his throat.

"What?" I can't stand the throat-clearing thing.

"Honey, there's one left in the cooler. Why don't you go ahead and take it before you go. I don't mind."

At times, when that wild urge comes over me *not* to slap his face, Brian can be a real sweetheart.

"I'm sorry if I'm being so awful. I'll make it up to you later, I promise." I say, stepping outside.

"Just be careful," he says, closing the door behind me.

Take Me to the River

Truth is in my heart, and in my breast there is neither craft nor guile. Grant thou that I may have my being among the living, and that I may sail up and down the river among those who are in thy following.

— from the *Egyptian Book of the Dead*

"On the day I was born, Daddy sat down and cried. Ma said I was born with the mark. Sure enough, when I was five years of age, I took up throwing knuckle bones. Grampa said what I had was a gift. The same gift he had been given from his pa. By the time I was seven, I knew gaming was in my blood." Anthony recites this bit of personal history while staring after a cloud of dust blowing from his gravel drive in the general direction of the river. It's a rare day when he feels long-in-the-face over his failure to inherit any of his father's urges to grub about in the soil or bake his back raw in the sun. Anthony's cousin, Oliver, spits between greasy engineer boots onto a couple of fire ants before leaning his chair back into the porch rail. He sucks at the end of a wooden match for a moment in thought.

"You're like one of them hounds, is what you are," Oliver says taking the match out of his mouth to speak. "Why, I bet you can smell the last coin in a man's pocket the day after payday."

Oliver often thinks of the palm reader he once saw in Memphis when he thinks of Anthony and his knack for gambling. It's like there's something going on that's beyond any logical explanation. It seems unlikely any one person could have been born with that much luck. Many of the men in town tend to agree with this notion and avoid Anthony Smith and his traveling deck of cards.

"Certainly on a poker night," Anthony says with a smile. He watches the dust cloud disappear into the distance. "Now, if I could only find a starter for my truck, I'd feel like the luckiest man in Luxora."

In the kitchen, Thelma is busy making egg salad for her afternoon visit with Reverend Johnson. She tells Anthony that she's been teaching the Reverend how to play rummy. Oliver watches her wrap sandwiches in wax paper out of the corner of his eye and remembers how, in sixth grade, Thelma had taught him the finer details of strip poker.

"While you and the Reverend are working a bit on the old religion thing," Anthony says looking into the refrigerator, "Oliver and I are going to be out some, hunting down a thing or two for the truck."

Thelma's second cousin is a pilot on one of the barges that U.S. Grain runs up and down the river. Anthony rarely misses the odd occasion when he would tie up in Osceola. For Anthony, the prospect of catching a free ride to points south or north is enough to warrant the three-and-a-half mile walk to port. Once, Anthony traveled all the way on up to Cairo just to spend a few days alone in thought on the Mississippi. Thelma does not understand Anthony's fascination with the river, but then again she's never stepped foot on a boat, either. Thelma seldom inquires as to Anthony's comings and goings.

Today, not quite an hour downstream of Osceola, Anthony makes himself comfortable on a heap of canvas piled between a couple of crates on a barge headed for West Memphis. He appears to doze off for a few minutes. At some point, while Oliver flips through the morning's *sports* section, Anthony opens his eyes and surveys the riverbank as it slowly slips by. He tosses a short length of straw into the water.

"Do you think Thelma will notice if you don't make it home tonight?" Oliver asks, watching the bit of straw float away in the murky water. Anthony picks at some sand on the canvas without responding as Oliver ruffles through a few pages and then stops to examine yesterday's results at Southland Park.

"Some people make a fair bit of cash on these dog races," Oliver says, pulling the paper close to his face. You'd think he was trying to smell the ink. Oliver immediately thinks of that little crystal beetle-bug Anthony keeps hidden in his hat. What Thelma calls a "skay-rab." His cousin said that it was like another eye for him, helped him to see how things will turn out in a game.

Anthony rubs his beard for a moment and looks up just in time to see a crane glide toward a small group of trees. He smiles and points, but says nothing. With his face buried in day-old greyhound statistics, Oliver misses the bird. Anthony leans back and closes his eyes.

"Those that go regular-like," Oliver continues, "they get to know the dogs pretty well. Just like Martin and David. Now, those boys sometimes do a fair bit better than eekin' out rent money. I've seen Martin walk away more than once with enough to get into the pyramid and watch them Pharaohs play."

"I thought Martin was on the dole," Anthony says, "so I don't see where making rent is all that big of a deal."

"Steady winning is impressive—and paying rent, even for that cheap little place of his, that ain't no small thing," Oliver says. Anthony shrugs, leans back into the canvas and closes his eyes again. Oliver tucks the newspaper under the canvas to keep it from blowing away and then makes himself comfortable. A short nap might not be such a bad idea. When his breathing begins to slow, Anthony stands and brushes the wrinkles from his pants. He bends down next to Oliver and carefully slips a folded up twenty dollar bill into his cousin's shirt pocket.

"I think it'd do me a bit of good to get out of Luxora for a couple of days," he says to himself, "the place smells like bad luck."

In the great state of Tennessee, the state legislature recently ratified a law which decrees that all public places shall post copies of the Ten Commandments. Gambling, much like country music, is taken very seriously in this part of the country, particularly in the city of Memphis. Unfortunately for the citizens of Memphis, there are also laws strictly prohibiting games of chance.

Now, it's common knowledge that games of chance are considered to include items such as slot machines, roulette wheels, cards and craps. Wagering on the Pharaohs is hardly a matter of chance, and when it comes to the question of track betting, well, Southland Park *is* in Arkansas.

Anthony has often contemplated the sad fact that the men of Memphis must flee to either Mississippi or Arkansas in order to enjoy the opportunity to try their hand at their favorite games. In West Memphis, these visiting cousins are partly responsible for Southland Park's success. In the past decade, the ripple effect of this success has triggered an economic impact of more than a half billion dollars on the state and local economy.

Anthony smiles to himself as he reads these very statistics from the sports page Oliver had tossed under the canvas. He cannot think of a day when he has personally realized any benefit from the state's supposed success. And yet he does smile to himself. Anthony counts himself among the blessed.

Martin and David spent the better part of the afternoon hanging about as close to the track as possible, hoping to pick up a few tips for the evening's races. Martin tells David he can read the trainers' lips as they lead the dogs onto the track and is certain he will be able to pin down better than half of the races with "Show" wagers. David pulls out a roll of twelve one-dollar bills from his pants pocket and surrenders them to Martin. "A man's got to do what a man's got to do," he tells himself, looking away from the track.

A half hour before post time, David notices Oliver on a bench across from an open betting window. He gives Martin's shirtsleeve a tug and points toward their friend.

"A sandwich and drink would be real nice 'bout now," Oliver says looking down from the tote board. Anthony shakes his head *no* without making a sound and continues to stare at the track. "We got lotsa time before . . ." Anthony raises his palm to quiet Oliver and shakes his head again.

When Martin and David greet Oliver, they slap him on the back fondly. Anthony takes a seat and examines the figures posted on the tote board as the three men talk about nothing in particular. After a few minutes, Oliver glances side to side looking for his cousin, and is surprised to find him sitting in a seat no more than a two feet away. "This here's Anthony Smith," he says. "He's my cousin I was telling you boys about."

Anthony's attention immediately leaves the board as he stands up to make the acquaintance of Oliver's friends. He offers them a smile, which seems perhaps a bit too familiar.

"Make yourselves comfortable," he offers the three men as he sits back down. "Oliver tells me you fellows are longtime veterans of the track. I've been looking at that scoreboard there figuring out which of these hounds is going to come in first place."

"Tote board," Martin says smiling, "and it's to *'Win.'*"

The four men talk about wagering in general and then discuss the day's favorites. After a few minutes, Oliver suggests they go on over to The Paddock Club, where they can order a nice dinner and keep their eyes on the dogs at the same time. Anthony stares at his cousin for a moment before he clasps his hands together and smiles at his boots.

"How about I pay for one of those tables with a television, and you," Anthony says looking up at Martin, "see if you can't find us some coffee."

At the finish of the first and second races, David and Martin shrug as they pocket their losing tickets and scribble notes on their race schedule. Oliver moans quietly to himself and scratches his head. At the finish of the third race, Oliver jumps out of his seat and throws his hat onto the table.

"*Reko Veto*!?" Oliver shouts, "I knew that puppy was going to win!" Martin looks at David and rolls his eyes. As Oliver sits back down and takes up arguing with Martin over this, Anthony excuses himself and wanders off toward the restrooms. When he returns five minutes later, Oliver is still ranting about the dog he should have wagered on.

"The fact is, cousin o' mine, you weren't so certain as to have made any bets," Anthony says sitting down.

"You know I ain't got no money," Oliver says.

"You got money," Anthony says.

"I ain't got nothin'."

"You got sixty for that cord of wood you hauled over to the Minseys' Saturday."

"It was forty, and that's long gone."

"I say it was sixty. You tucked twenty of it into your shirt for later," Anthony says, looking toward the track.

Oliver draws a twenty from his shirt pocket. "Guess I clean forgot about that. Thanks, cuz—aww, now that really does it!" Oliver says throwing the bill onto the table, "I'd be going home a rich man had I known!"

Anthony leans forward and flips a pair of one dollar bills onto the table. "There's your winnings, Oliver," he says, "*Reko Veto* won for even money. Two dollar ticket is a two dollar win."

"I'd a' bet twenty," Oliver says pushing the bills back. Anthony takes the money and hands it to David.

"What do you think, David? Would my cousin here have bet twenty?"

"Why I believe he would have," David says, smiling. "Oliver isn't the sort to say he would've if he didn't mean it."

Anthony rubs his beard for a moment and then shoves his hand into his trousers pocket. "I suppose it's your lucky day then," he says, holding a twenty out to Oliver, "It just so happens I made good on that race, and being the honest soul that I am, I feel down right amicable to sharing in the winnings. Seeing's how you'd a bet your wad, so to speak."

"Hah!" Oliver says, grabbing the twenty. "Tony, I always said you're a better man than me. You see there, boys, you ain't gonna find a more upright fella anywhere near 'bouts."

"You wagered on that race?" Martin asks, watching Oliver push the money into his shirt pocket.

"You know it," Anthony says. "Boxed trifecta. The other two hounds were at five and nine."

"How'd you do that?" Oliver asks, looking around the table with a puzzled look.

"Ah, you were in the can," Anthony says, looking Oliver in the eye.

"How did you do on the first two races?" David asks.

"I only bet on that one race," Anthony says, "It's the only race my system guaranteed me to win."

"System, hah! You think you got yourself a system there bud?" Martin says, slapping his knee, "Those so-called systems ain't squat. Unless you know your dogs, you ain't got nothing but some kinda luck."

"As I said, boy," Anthony says, smiling, "one ticket is all I needed. It's not like I bet on a whole slew o' races."

"Boy, Boy? Who are *you* calling a *boy*? Why . . . why . . ." David stammers.

"Hold on," Martin says patting David on the back, "maybe the man's got something there."

"That I do," Anthony says folding his hands. "What I have is a surefire system handed down from ancient times, or so my pappy told me."

"Why, sure he does," Oliver says. "My cousin here is winning all sorts of stuff with that system there of his."

"So saith Anthony," Martin says with a sideways glance at Oliver, "You make it sound like your system is something you read off of some golden tablets. Maybe you got it written down in a book someplace."

"Oh, but I will!" Anthony laughs.

With surprisingly little effort, Anthony convinces the three men to abandon their evening at the dog track for a rather lengthy meal at a nearby diner.

What is to follow comes in the shape of secret handshakes and knowing looks among a small group of men amidst crowds of common gamblers. The unwary stare at the ever-changing tote board before pushing their way toward open betting windows. Indeed, it *does* begin here. Once, even I overheard a discussion between two men in which one of the fellows claimed to be a personal friend of Anthony's, or at least he'd once stood next to his cousin in line and had picked up on a winning tip. The stories of Anthony at the track seemed to grow with time.

What we do know is that something in the order of thirty-four thousand copies of the book *A Gentlemen's Discourse on Greyhound Racing*, written by one A. Smith and published by M. Harris & Associates, were sold within two years following that first meeting of Anthony and Martin. Shortly after its first printing, Anthony virtually stopped going to the dog track. Rumor has it that he began to invest much of the money from the sales of this book in the law office Oliver did janitorial work in. This law office specialized in the lucrative field of personal injury. The return on Anthony's investment was substantial, to say the least.

Martin, on the other hand, did not do nearly so well. It was with his winnings from a Pick Six that the group of men had financed the publication of this "gambling guide." With the exception of Anthony, he was actually receiving the largest percentage of profits from its sales. And while Martin had something of an affinity for back alley card games, he always swore by Anthony's wagering system and the dog track in general. It was later discovered by David that Martin had squandered his savings playing slot machines in a casino somewhere up river.

What we do *not* know, and what all of the known stories fail to tell us, is how on one certain spring morning Anthony Smith wandered on foot from Luxora to Osceola. He followed the river without any apparent reason other than perhaps to watch the rising sun's reflection on its brown face. And as unlikely as it might seem, Anthony caught a ride on the *Memphis Queen* as it passed dutifully along on its run from Cairo to Mud Island. Of course, anyone who has ever pulled all sevens or won the lottery can tell you that *anything* is possible.

On the deck behind the steering house, Anthony seated himself at a small table of glass and green, painted wrought iron. It only seemed natural that he should find himself playing cards once more with his brother, Abe. This is the son the Smith family had long since forgotten. He disappeared from Luxora onto the river some years past with little more than the shoes on his feet and a funny pair of dice in his pocket. In his heart, Anthony suspected that Abe hoped to jump ship some day if he could ever get ahead by more than a couple of coins. Perhaps then he might make it somewhere on the other side of the river.

"So tell us my good brother," Abe said, "what exactly were you thinking when you and your friends saw fit to send to print that illustrious manuscript you have laid claim to?"

"I'm not sure what you're talking about there, Abe," Anthony said, fanning out the cards in his hand.

"What I am referring to is your so-called guide to the ponies."

"Hounds."

Abe produced a copy of the book from his vest pocket. "Whatever you say Anthony; but the fact of the matter is this; it was ponies when I wrote the thing."

"Are you calling me a liar, Abe? I got myself three friends who'll swear I done wrote that all on my own."

"Be that as it may, you and I both know better." Abe laid the book on the table. "I should have figured it out early on, why you seemed to steer me towards discourse on thoroughbreds."

"Steer what?" Anthony said, a bit puzzled.

"To get me to talk at length about racehorses," Abe said without a hint of sarcasm.

"You know it wasn't your system, anyhow. It was Gramps, and that makes it just as much mine as yours," Anthony said putting his cards down on top of the book.

"The system did not belong to our dear grandfather, either. It's the work of several generations of careful study of human behavior."

"Like I said Abe, it ain't yours."

"I am; however, the author of the manuscript we see here before us. And the truth is, there are other people beside myself who are very disappointed that you have taken such liberties. To some extent, I have already had to answer for your actions. I do believe they would like to take up this point of contention with you within the next few days."

"I ain't going to be talkin' to any of *your* friends."

"I would not lay any wagers on that one, brother," Abe said. He sat for a moment, staring quietly at the passing banks. "There is something I would like you to listen to before you go."

"What's that, Abe?"Anthony asked looking off toward the river also.

"This morning, there, on the horizon," Abe said pointing toward the port side of the boat, "the first sliver of the sun shot across the black lands and reflected off calm water. The sun leaped out of the netherworld and into the sky. It seemed only a moment for a full golden disk to appear and make the fields all around green. This early morning green cannot be described or seen anywhere in the world but here, on these mornings. As the sun climbed the horizon, the dark water of the river boiled as fish began to stir. The harmony of the sun, green fields and water were glorious. It is on mornings such as this I know that my heart truly belongs here, in the black lands."

Anthony looked away from the shore and at his brother, who sat there with something like a smile on his face. "That's great, Abe," he said tipping his hat, "just . . . great." Anthony then gathered up the cards from the table and went downstairs to the lower deck. The *Memphis Queen* was about to dock and he had a bus to catch.

When Anthony Smith checked into the Carthage Inn later that day, he had no idea how soon it would be before he was to see Abe again.

In the Kingdom of the Blind

Tell me what you see.

I can't see anything, I already told you that. I'm just lying here feeling the spread of calm.

You lie. I know that you can see. You're sitting on a ledge. You're sitting on the rock wall which divides these two fields. I'm here in this field of wheat. Look to the other side and tell me what you see.

I see nothing.

You lie.

Why should I?

You're sitting on a wall. Do you understand?

Yes.

What do you see?

Where?

The other side. What's on the other side?

I can't see anything. Don't you understand? I think I may be blind. Why did I ever let you do this to me?

We agreed to this, now look.

I see nothing. Explain why I'm here. Please, I've forgotten.

It's your time to climb over. I shall never be able to make the climb myself. You promised to let me know what's there.

Why can't you come over?

No soul.

I can't understand.

I have no soul.

You do, I know you do.

No.

You must.

None.

But I've always thought yours to be the most beautiful.

I'm sorry, but this is all I am. Perhaps I already exist as a soul. That might be why I can't climb to where you are. Now, pay attention. You have already shown me that you're on a rock wall.

Have I?

You have.

Oh, I'd forgotten.

Tell me.

I can smell.

Smell? What do you smell?

Music. It tastes wonderful.

Do you smell it or taste it? Which?

Yes.

Do you smell or taste the music?

Yes.

Damn you. Can you understand me?

Yes. I can't see anything, so stop torturing me.

Forget what there is to see. Show me the music.

It's sweet and the sky's blue. I taste that also. And clouds . . .

Can you taste these?

What?

The clouds.

Yes.

Show me.

I'm floating. They're white. Below, the field is green. I had thought it would be black. It doesn't smell that way at all. The sky's colder than the ledge. I must float.

Wait. Show me the field.

What?

The green field. Is this something you smell, or can you see that it's green?

When?

The field! I really didn't think this would be so difficult. God Almighty!

Yes?

Can you show me anything of the field?

Where's the child?

Don't worry about that now. Show me the field.

I can't. What have you done?

I ended the pain. Now show me.

I won't.

Alright, do you remember the promise I made? To watch over the child?

You did?

I did. Don't you remember?

Maybe.

You do remember. I have always been here. I shall never leave.

I remember. You have always been there. You shall never leave.

Now, the field.

What should I say? I'm here. I sit in the middle of a field of wild grass. As far as I can tell, it's in all directions. This place is without trees of any kind. There are no trees here either. The field is green. There are no trees, but there is water. The sky's sweet. It's blue. The field's green and the sky's blue. Can you understand this? This isn't their color, it's what they are. The clouds are white.

Do you see these things?

How can I? I've already told you that I'm blind. This one before me, the hands, the eyes.

What, is someone there with you?

Your eyes. I've missed you. Can you help me off with this?

Wait . . .

Thank you. That was heavy. Oh my, it's beautiful here.

Tell me what you see.

I've no eyes. Stop asking.

Tell me something—please.

Yes. Do you promise?

I do.

Then I'm gone.

No, that's not fair. We had a deal.

There was never a deal. To you it's a hideous thought that I could ever be happy. I am now, thank you.

I can't bring you back.

I know that.

I've lost you.
Yes.
Are you there?
I'm green,
Tell me.
I'm blue,
Are you there?
I'm white . . .

Fish Tales

I know that it's Sarah who's been on the tip of things these last few nights as I'd sit up in bed covered in sweat. Each time I've been startled enough by strange dreams, I get up for a while and wander about some. Usually, I'll go sit in the kitchen so I can look out the window. Sometimes I go look into the empty field out back. After a few minutes, I'll go back to bed and lie down. I don't usually remember closing my eyes, but I always fall right back to sleep.

I was pretty surprised this morning, when Aunt Edna flashed a little smile at me just after catching me staring down the neck of Sarah's blouse as she was scraping eggs off her plate into Shep's bowl. I'm not real sure what her smiling was trying to tell me just then, but one thing's for sure—I needed to get out of that house for a bit. What I needed to do was some thinking. Right after lunch, I grabbed my pole from out of the workshop and headed down to Dicle Creek with Shep.

I've been thinking how I ought to probably be sorting out this whole business about Sarah and Steve. None of it ever made a bit of sense anyhow. Well, I suppose I shouldn't be thinking of her the way I've been lately, anyway. Not like that, anyhow. It probably isn't right. It doesn't really much matter though, because this morning I'm kind of worried about something else.

What's been bothering me is how things have just sort of been happening. Things which just seem to go on by accident. They've been happening after I say things in this kind of kidding sort of way. This has been going on for some time now, but I haven't breathed a word of it to anyone. Not lately, anyhow. The first time was something like a year ago. I was in town getting a new manifold for the truck and thought it'd be kind of funny to play a joke on Mr. Ryder at the feed store. It wasn't meant to be a mean-spirited joke. Just something harmless. I couldn't help but think how it'd be a real side splitter. What I did was I told Mr. Ryder how Ben Stowell was going to come by in an hour or so to pick up five hundred pounds of laying mash. Mr. Ryder's eyebrows raised, a bit skeptical like, at this. He knew, just like I did, that the Stowell's coop had burnt down a long time ago, and they'd just sold their remaining hens to Barton Farms. The joke was on me, though, because when I walked past Ryder's side yard a couple hours later, I saw Ben apologizing for showing up an hour late as he tossed the last bag of mash into the back of his pickup.

At the time, I thought that was about the weirdest thing that I ever heard of, something being so coincidental like that. Heck, it was for sure the strangest thing that ever happened to me. I told a couple people about it shortly after, but nobody seemed to believe me, so I just kind of forgot about the whole thing for a while.

I started thinking about that again after I stopped by Mike's place to watch a ball game one Sunday afternoon. During a commercial, I said something like it was too bad about the back of his car being smashed in and all. Well, Mike had just bought a brand new Mustang, and I thought this wisecrack would send him running because he loved that new white convertible more than his wife, Barbara, or even his dog.

"Yeah, right, Toby." he said, and didn't even budge off the couch.

"Holy cow! Mike, you better get out there," Barbara said, staring out the livingroom window.

I got up to take a look outside and sure enough, there was this huge Ford LTD nosed right into the back of Mike's car. Some guy in coveralls was bouncing on the front of it, like he was trying to break something loose.

It didn't take but a half second for me to remember that time at the feed store. I may not be real bright, but I can sure add two and two pretty quick. That whole scene at Mike's was way too much for me, so I left Mike and Barbara to sort things out themselves. I went home kind of wondering if maybe I was like a freak or something.

That was about a month ago, and I've been doing a lot of thinking since. This afternoon I thought maybe what I'd do is just kind of think things out. One thing at a time, you know. About a week ago, I said something joking-like again, only this time it was deliberate-like, just to see what would happen. I won't say what it was I said, but I scared the hell out of myself. So now I've been worrying about this a lot the last few days. I guess the thing about Steven marrying Sarah also bothers me some. I can't figure why though. I shouldn't ought to think of her like that. Anyway, I thought maybe snagging a couple bullhead would help me think things out quietly, one thing at a time, you know.

Creek's a good place to go if you've got to think about things. Good place to go and not think about stuff too. I like the slow, dark water. I just lay back and watch Shep as he runs about wildly, scaring up birds. This afternoon, though, I thought I'd actually try to catch something. That'd help maybe so I could just think about one thing at a time.

I thought I'd start by floating a pinky out a ways with a shingle and then tug it off over a hole. I caught a monster last summer doing it like that. I forgot to grab a bit of shingle coming out of the workshop, so I thought I'd improvise with a short stub of a branch. Keeping the pinky on this branch was near to impossible, so I tossed that to look for some bark. After a couple of minutes, I had a piece that worked pretty good. I floated it to the other side of a little jetty where there was a spot that the bed had been sucked off by the water. I tugged the little guy off and then watched him go down. Line began to pay out with the flow for a bit. I let it drag out loose for a while. The pinky came to a stop and the line on the surface started to pile up. I quickly began to reel up the loose stuff before it'd start getting tangled. Before I had it all, the slack went out on it's own and I could feel the pinky getting dragged out and then it stopped. I started to pull back real hard because I was sure I had something. Well, I was pulling and pulling and pretty soon I figured I was just hung up on something. I started to whip the end of my pole forward and back hoping it would give way. At one point, the pinky got pulled out some more real hard. I knew that I wasn't just snagged up on a rock or something. I pulled some more, but pretty soon it began to feel like it was just that. A rock.

I sat there for about an hour hoping whatever bit onto my gizzy would do something. The sun was going to start waving goodbye, so I needed to do something soon. I was just about to start whipping my pole about some more when my line went completely limp. The line broke on its own. Just then, I was startled by a voice not more than a foot or two behind me.

"What'd ya think there, Toby?"

I turned about to find Ralph standing there with this big smile on his face. Ralph is this old guy that lives on a big farm about a half mile down the creek. I told him that I just lost the biggest bullhead of my life, or maybe that I had just been hung up on nothing. Ralph said it sounded like a bullhead, but not to worry, I'll get him soon. Ralph and I sat down on the bank and watched the sun fall the rest of the way into the hills. Shep lay in some tall grass nearby, exhausted.

I had taken off my boots while we were sitting there and was cooling off my toes in the water. I was thinking about maybe telling Ralph about how I thought things I kid around about just seem to happen. Would he think I'm crazy? Maybe its like a Houdini trick he could explain to me or something. Well, I was going to ask when he shouts all of the sudden.

"Grab 'em, Toby!"

I look down at my feet in time to see this huge lunker about to go for my foot. I gill the thing and heave it up onto the bank. It was absolutely huge, maybe thirty pounds.

"God Almighty!" I said, as I spotted a short bit of line hanging out of the thing's mouth. "That's the one!"

Ralph just laughed and shook his head. Then he gave me a good, hard slap on the back and began to walk off. As he walked off, he said something and then threw up a hand in a quick wave. I couldn't hear what he'd said, and I suddenly felt it might be something I'd want to hear.

"What was that Ralph?" I shouted at his back. He repeated whatever it was and threw up his hand again. I still didn't hear what he'd said. I ran up after him a few steps and shouted again. This time Ralph shouts back over his shoulder.

"Shame 'bout Steve, huh, Toby? What'd ya say?"

I kind of just stood there for a moment with my mouth hanging open like a dutch door. Ralph stopped and turned around to look at me, fists set on hips. After a couple moments of staring through me, he cupped his hand around his mouth like a megaphone so I could hear him plain this time,

"Boy, grab yer fish an' bring 'em here. There's somethin' I need to show ya."

Mourning for Margaret

Whoever you are: in the evening step out
of your room, where you know everything;
yours is the last house before the far-off:
whoever you are.

from "Entrance"
—*Rainer Maria Rilke*

Monday

It is difficult to understand how I came to exist here. Yet while I exist in the middle of the desert, I do not consider this home.

During the summer, a fine dust gets into everything. The wind never stops and this dust works its way into every corner. It does not matter where things are hidden, nothing is sacred.

The desert summer seems intent on paralyzing thought. Its heat numbs the mind. It kills. In this heat, small things perish. Things whose existence is fragile. I believe love to be fragile, though it is often no small thing. Poets have proclaimed love to be all things: patient, enduring, faithful, sometimes bitter. As I look on the dust which pervades this place, my heart proclaims love to be fragile. It is necessary that I proclaim it so, or what I must now relate means nothing.

The desert winter numbs the soul, freezes feeling. Here, there are no snowy sceneries to mask the dirt and weeds which lie in all directions. No rains. Winter is hard. If snow comes, it is like a snow of death. Snow white, this snow falls black. There are only two seasons, summer and winter.

I have been told this desert lies within a valley. Incredulous tales—I see no valley. In all directions, the horizon is consumed with the dwellings of other souls. Dens of thieves. The desert is flat and desolate with no relief. Above these dwellings no crest of mountain or hill may be seen. Desolate all. To the south, just above the roof of a dwelling, is the rough silhouette of some mountainous peak as large as any. Why, its foot lies before me. I am at its very foot. I am its foot. This dwelling is its doorstep.

Tuesday

It is cold early in the morning. Not so cold as to frost roofs or freeze one's breath. It is an empty cold. A quiet calm. The chill of darkness. In the east, the sun has yet to show her face.

I enter the doorway. My eyes rise above me. They take in this mountain upon which I must climb. I want this mountain to be my home. The beauty of it overwhelms, its face made green by the streams which course down it. My journey begins.

I proceed along the path which springs from this doorstep. This path immediately begins upward. One path may become many and lead to all places. This path, however, must lead only to one route. All of those other paths, leading to all of those other places, do not exist for me. This is the only path which will take me to the summit. Is God there? Who is this eavesdropping on these thoughts? Are you God? Perhaps, assuming each of us is punctual, we may share some water on the summit.

The path is empty. No dwellings or souls as it gradually ascends the mountain. Wheels, broken fences, leaves of papers, read and unread, tombstones, long and broad. These flat stones are weatherworn, and the chiseled word no longer legible. Dead tombstones.

I follow the ascending path carefully. As I follow, the sun rises. Her face touches mine. In the morning, there is no wind or sand. The sun looks on with her bright, yellow face. Later in the evening, she will be red. That red face is one of a long life. Strange, my attire is all in gray.

As the sun travels the sky, I find that this path is a less difficult task than I had imagined it to be. I slow my pace, then halt. I look on what I have accomplished. It does not seem as though I have traveled far, yet it is obvious that the desert below lies within a valley. The desert below is like the face of some other world, masked in a haze of filth. Perhaps this is only dust, or sand which has been swept up into the air by wind. That cannot be right, the land itself is dirty. Dwellings are arranged randomly. The landscape is filled with an immense collection of refuse which cannot be imagined, let alone described. There are entire hills which appear to be composed of refuse.

Lower on this path I had perceived the desert as some sort of graveyard. No more than a desolate place filled with quiet and death. Gazing downward, I realize that this may not be. The desert below appears to be little more than a garbage dump.

Having stopped, I take the opportunity to spend a few moments looking around. Along this stretch of path, the landscape does not appear to be as green and lush as it had appeared from below. I turn and gaze toward where I imagine the summit to be. The landscape in that direction seems greener. Perhaps I am not actually on the mountain proper yet. The vegetation here is short and full of thorns. Litter dots the hills here, though it appears to be more selective. Though refuse abounds, there is much less than what is present in the desert below. It may be that its appearance is accentuated by the surrounding environment. One could suffocate in filth down in the desert. Here, alongside the path, this trash appears as the clutter of children.

I turn to face the mountain. I continue this journey. Before me, the path makes a sudden steep incline, which appears to run forever upward. I exert a great effort in order to continue. I am uncertain if I can continue. Perhaps if I spoke to myself. Some words of encouragement. I know I can. I falter. It is ridiculous to think at all. I should not think. Not now.

Suddenly, I am here on the mountain. This place is beautiful. I understand what it is that I must do to make an ascension such as this. Having reached this apex here along the path, I shall stop and return to the desert. I am not prepared to attain the summit today. I know I am incapable of accomplishing this in single a journey. I have spent a considerable portion of the day achieving so little.

I rapidly descend the path. I look back on the rising path and contemplate why I did not continue for a little while more. The day is only half over. Looking toward the mountain, I regret the decision to turn back.

Later from my doorstep, the sun sets.

Wednesday

Another day. I am often surprised when I open my eyes and discover it is just that. Today, I think I should repeat my attempt to reach the summit of this mountain. I have discovered a great secret. I think back on the effort as I progressed along that path and recall pleasure. Though I failed to reach the summit, I realize that it was the journey, the climb itself, which provided satisfaction.

I enter the doorway. My eyes rise above me. They rise and take in this mountain upon which I must climb. The path does not cut through the mountain's beauty and scar it. As it ascends the face, it becomes cloaked by forest and the immensity of the mountain. The path does not appear to be even insignificant. It does not appear.

It is with intent that I begin. The path is the same as it was yesterday. I notice alongside the path, to the left, an immense pile of leaves lying beneath an ancient tree. Strange, I do not recall either the leaves or the tree on yesterday's journey. As I continue past this pile of leaves I stare into them. I wonder how it is that I could have missed something so large, so entirely noticeable. Perhaps my eyes or thoughts were elsewhere.

By mid-morning, I near the place where yesterday's journey ended. Little effort was required to come to this place now. Yesterday had seemed so difficult. I remember that I doubted myself.

I stop to look down on the desert. It seems unrealistic somehow. This place, this path crawling up the face of the mountain, this is real. It is green and wet. Below I see only emptiness. Dead is how it appeared yesterday. I wonder, is the view the same? I believe it is.

I continue my journey. Within a short time, I pass that place where I had stopped before. Having only just started, I do not even slow my pace, but continue forward full of encouragement. Within a short time the path levels and becomes flat. At this point, traveling becomes effortless. I become uncertain in which direction the path progresses, since it no longer runs straight; nor does it remain visible for any distance as it disappears into the forest. As I look toward the mountain's summit I cannot discern whether the path runs up the face in some winding manner or wraps around the mountain in one direction or the other. Only the path knows its own future.

Late morning. I have reached a point where the path appears to end. It connects in a perpendicular fashion with another path which runs east-west. Maybe this path does not end. Certainly this new path is intended as a continuation of the path on which I stand. This must be the path I must travel.

I had not anticipated choices. Pure determination and effort. I am concerned that whichever path I pursue could lead me astray. To the right, the path appears to slowly bend deeper into the forest. The left course appears to run either away from the mountain or perhaps around it. I follow the path west. After navigating the very first bend, the path makes a rapid ascension, which appears to be at a nearly impossible incline. I quickly discover that the effort required to ascend hardly any distance at all, to a point only slightly further along the path, is so great that I am spending a large portion of the day traveling no distance at all.

Late afternoon. Finally I have reached a small crest in the path. To the right, there is a small clearing. A widening in the path as though intended as a place of rest. This small clearing chews into a hillside, and from the path, there is nothing to view except the path itself as it disappears in either direction. As I look around, I guess it is often frequented. The evidence is in the form of more refuse. Empty wine bottles, tattered pieces of printed matter and bits of clothing are strewn everywhere.

I approach the edge of this clearing to one side of the damaged hill. From here I can look down on the desert and its flatness. I can see that the path here will actually run away from the mountain. This clearing is on some lower crest in the path.

As I leave the clearing's edge and return to the path, I notice a pile of discarded decorations from some forgotten celebration or festival. I wonder if someone was celebrating their quest up this mountain. If this were so, then they obviously did not see it looming behind them. Maybe this was the only summit they ever desired to attain. The air is still. In the distance, there is the caw of a raven.

To no great surprise, the path rapidly winds in a direction away from the mountain and steeply descends toward the desert. I pass through landscape which seems far more barren than that place where I dwell. The refuse here seems strange. Stone and crooked bits of wood. Flowers jabbed into shallow earth.

You are dust.

As I approach the last tombstone on the left, I recognize a familiar path which should soon return me to my abode. Following this path toward the right, I find that I am not too late for supper.

Thursday

It is cold in the early morning. In the east, the sun has not yet risen. My neighbors appear only in shades of gray. Do I repeat the ritual? A tradition whose roots strain toward yesterday. Follow the steps, the gestures, those sacred thoughts God has whispered into my ear.

Follow the path. My quest is for a wonderful place. I know this path. I will retrace yesterday's steps, and this time, I will follow the correct path. I will know which is the right path. I shall not look back. If I am to gain the top of this mountain, I cannot look back.

I enter the doorway. My eyes rise above me. They rise and take in this mountain upon which I must climb. My eyes are intent upon the path which lies beneath my feet. Intent as I pass over it. Every inch is sharp and contrasting. Individual stones and bits of glass. Suddenly, I look up. I am momentarily given start by the presence of an immense pile of leaves beneath an ancient tree. Is this yesterday's tree? The events of yesterday seem so unimportant. I wonder if they were just as unimportant yesterday. The path passing below is what is significant. Not the path. This journey has become significant. My presence on the path.

It is mid-morning when I reach the point of division in the path. The sun shines bright. The path leads away, right and left. I follow the left as I had intended. For a short distance, the path veers away from the mountain and descends rapidly. It seems incredible to imagine that all my effort, all my progress so far, will be rapidly undone. Descent requires no effort and takes very little time. At the bottom of the slope, the path makes a sharp twist and heads back toward the mountain.

I find myself within a small circular valley. This place is so small that perhaps it should not be considered a proper valley. Three routes appear to lead out of the valley and toward the summit. Of the paths confronting me, I have no means of discerning which will actually lead to the summit. As a continuation of this day's journey, I follow the left tract.

Before continuing, I must stop. This valley seems to be a place of rest. Refuse everywhere. Can beauty not be left alone?

The path here is difficult. The effort of ascent forces thoughts to follow behind; they follow ahead. My mind searches this path. There is something about the path here, something different. The refuse here seems more natural. It is in the form of stone. Collections of stones large and small line the path. These stones seem to have been assembled deliberately. I do not understand the intent of these monuments in miniature. The stones must have been dumped here. I wonder if they have been left to be rid of. Perhaps they, too, have lost their meaning.

I ask myself why. Certainly those who left these piles are long gone from this place. If the stones have been forgotten, they no longer belong to anyone.

Before this path bends away further from the mountain, it runs into yet another path which runs directly up the face of the mountain. Looking toward the desert, this new path seems to continue straight. Perhaps this is the middle path from the valley. But then again, this may be some new path. If it is, it ends before it reaches the desert, otherwise I would have crossed it during my journey. I do not believe paths end traveling downhill. All paths lead to the desert. I believe only one reaches the summit.

I stop in the middle of this path as though I have forgotten where I am. Looking around, I see nothing but the forested mountainside. Somewhere, not too far off, a robin sings.

It is late in the afternoon. I should return. As I begin to descend, I notice a large mound of bricks lying next to the path. Not a pile of stone. Brick. It is likely that this mound may be greater than all of the stones which line this path, should they be piled together in a single mound.

I descend, past all of the stones which have been lined to stare, perhaps to encourage, the work of those who come this way. Perhaps to discourage. I travel through the small valley, leaving behind the other paths which must be explored another day. Downward.

As I pass the ancient tree alongside the path, not far from where I dwell, I stop for a moment and stare at the leaves which lie beneath it. I wish to run through these leaves and kick them into the air. To lie down with them. If I do, I fear I might not rise again. I continue down the path.

It does not seem late, and yet as I approach my doorstep, the sun sets.

Friday

Again, it is cold. To the east, the sky is red. The sun has begun to rise. The desert is dressed in scarlet. I am drawn to the mountain. I am to make this journey. This is what I am to do. Without looking, I move forward. The path lies before me.

I enter the doorway. My eyes rise above me. They take in this mountain upon which I must climb. I move past the leaves, the ancient tree. Everything seems to be in order. Shall I march? My goal remains the same. I shall walk. I ascend with ease. I almost could not make it this far on the first journey. Past the division in the path. Onward to the small valley.

And here where the paths converge, I find that I am confronted with the two paths which remain. The path which is straight and lies between the right and left, and the path which lies to the right.

I no longer believe that I travel this path only for the sake of travel. My desire has an end. I desire the greatest height this mountain offers. I ascend the path on the right.

This path I follow is the most unusual thus far. It is rocky and steep. The rocks are not littered alongside the path. They are in the path itself. Some lie loose in the path, while others are embedded in the path and protrude; some create obstacles which may be tripped over if not carefully looked for. I must watch the path carefully here or I am certain to fall. The path seems to have come to this condition either from much overuse and no maintenance or from a total absence of use. Between the jagged stones is dust. An extremely fine dust which puffs beneath feet, leaving a small cloud behind as I travel.

This dusty path seems a paradox. The forest here is beautiful. It is green and lush. There must be water nearby. To my surprise, the path flattens out for a short distance. Further up, it continues its steep ascent. But here, unseen from a dozen paces behind, the path is level. Cutting through the path at a right angle is a small stream, perhaps three paces wide. Probably no more than ankle deep at its center. What a wonderful relief! I wade to the center of the stream and cool my feet. Looking about for a rock or log to sit on, I find none. I have a long distance to travel today and it has become warm. I sit in the middle of the stream. Looking downward, I can see I have traveled high enough to see the desert below. Actually, what I see is the cloud of dust that covers it. I am startled by the sound of a bird. A fluttering of wings. A small white bird, apparently intent on bathing in the stream, changes its plans after nearly landing on my head. The foolish bird in its fright flies toward the desert.

It would be wonderful to stay here. Not ascend or descend. Just to sit in cool water. Time to go. It is beyond late morning, and if I am to progress, I must stand and walk.

As I ascend the path, I realize that dust sticks to my wet feet. Not sticking, but caking on to a thickness which hinders progress. The further I travel the heavier my feet become. Stepping forward, I kick my right foot into a stone in the path, hoping to dislodge some of this mud. I succeed in knocking loose some of the mud, but I also trip over the stone and stumble. No harm really. The path is soft and I did not fall on any of the rocks which are so abundant. As a result of falling, I am covered in mud and a thin layer of dust. Had I not sat in the stream, I would only be covered in dust. Instead, my entire backside is now mud. As I continue to ascend, I attempt to brush away the mud. I manage to loosen some of it, but have managed to muddy my hands and arms for good measure.

In a short time I dry out, and the mud falls from me, leaving my apparel filthy. I stop to take inventory. There is no point in returning. It is not as though I need to be presentable. I shall remain gray with dust no matter what. If I begin to descend, I shall only come back tomorrow so that I can continue this journey.

This path is different from yesterday's. It is different because the refuse here is absent. Though the path itself is in disrepair, it appears that some effort has been made to keep this path free from the refuse so prevalent in the desert below. But for all the refuse which must have been removed, there is an overwhelming presence of those things which could never be removed: slivers of broken glass, and bits of torn paper. Small things which cannot be collected.

Shortly, I find myself in a wide open area—which the path has become. The relentless ascent has stopped, and all around is an open flat area in the middle of the forest. It is circular and for the most part enclosed by trees. The trees watch over this place, but cannot come forward. A portion of this place, which is not enclosed by the forest, lies directly in front of me. From where I am, it seems there might be a steep drop. Perhaps a cliff. Beyond this edge, through unmeasured space, lies the top of the mountain.

From out of the trees comes a man. He walks directly toward me. He smiles and walks past me. In one hand, he grasps a wooden rod which serves as the handle for a wooden box that is overfilled with various hand tools. Under his arms are wooden stakes and planks. Reaching the path, he drops the lumber and the box of tools. Reaching into the box, he grabs a mallet. He pounds one end of a stake into the ground. I turn to the mountain. I cross the open area to the edge. From this edge, I am able to view the entirety of what remains to be seen of the mountain. Looking down, I see a path which seems quite straight. Connecting to it on the opposite side from where I am looking is another path. I study this for sometime and realize this is the path I followed yesterday. I think I can see the pile of brick.

Looking at the points on the paths below and at the mountain before me, I guess that I am perhaps half again the distance to the summit. I also perceive a number of other plateaus below. Some may be at the same elevation as where I now stand. Some are higher. Perhaps there are also paths which lead to these places. Where would these other paths come from? The more I look, the more routes I see. It is no wonder this place is spoiled with refuse. Civilization is everywhere.

Turning from the mountain before me, I look toward the path from where I have just come. A few paces away is a large pile of palm fronds. This pile is so high I imagine they must be intended for a fire rather than refuse. I return to the path.

As I approach the clearing's edge, I observe what this man has been working on. It is a sign. With a final pound, he drives the final nail into a short post. In large red letters this sign is intended to indicate a path which leads to the summit of the mountain. The sign, however, points toward the desert. Staring at me, the man smiles for a moment.

"It is finished," he mumbles to his feet. He then collects his tools and wanders off toward the trees.

I discount blindness and maliciousness. This man must be without sense, or is of the sort of humor few would appreciate. Perhaps he is just lost. Behind me, from the clearing, I hear the caw of some bird. Stepping forward, I begin my descent.

Descending this path is as difficult as ascending others. This fine powder of dust makes it difficult to walk with the sure footing required to descend with confidence. The rocks are difficult to see at each step. Rocks tip and roll beneath my feet, causing me to stumble. I arrive at the stream without falling.

I do not believe that it has been long since I was last here, and yet water no longer flows across the path. The path is wet with mud. In places, small puddles shine scarlet with the reflection of the lowering sun. I retreat several steps and estimate the distance to the other side. With my best start, I am not capable of leaping across. Perhaps I could just run at the mud, and when I reach it, I could leap on it and hope to skim across its surface to the other side. I could flap my arms. I take another step back. Actually, the only way across is to walk as carefully as possible and take what mud may come. On the other side, I will remove it as best I can.

I approach the mud and place my right foot into the wet silt. My foot shoots forward. I fall back, but before becoming engulfed, I put down one hand to catch myself. I stand back up. My hand is weighted with an unusually thick layer of mud.

I proceed across the stream. Another two steps and I am almost to the opposite side. The mud is more than ankle deep and my feet become stuck. As I twist my body toward the right attempting to pull a foot free, I notice that just off the path lies a small formation of rocks which create a path across the stream bed. I step out from the mud.

On the dry path, my muddy feet collect dust. Within a few steps, they become so heavy that I can barely lift them. Staggering, I move toward the rocks so I may sit and remove the mud. I look for a stick—or perhaps a small rock—which I may use as a scraper. I find neither. Using an already muddied hand, I try to remove as much of this mud as I can. The more I try to remove it, the more mud I end up with on my hand. Finally, I have to use my clean hand to squeeze off some of the mud on the other.

I hope this mud will dry and break off during my descent. Traveling down this path becomes a nightmare. I doubt I can make it. My limbs are so heavy I have lost all control. I merely stumble downward. I no longer control steps or balance if I happen on some waiting rock. I am exhausted to the point of feeling I must stop where I am. Perhaps I can rest; sleep until tomorrow. Sleep and not wake. I wish only to rest. I no longer wish to know of summits or the paths which lead to them. I want to stop; end it here. I do not care where or when I am. Let me sleep.

I sleep alongside the path. Snug and warm. Sleep without dreams. This is a quiet, calm sleep. I lie here unaware. A hand lies on my heart. That hand shakes and I wake. It is not yet completely dark. I am uncertain how long I have lain here. Bewildered, I look about to determine where I am. To my surprise, I find that I have fully descended the mountain. As I pick myself up, I find that I had lain down amidst the large pile of leaves under the ancient tree. Asleep among leaves.

Though it is not completely dark, the sun has set and dinner is long past. As I approach my house, I wonder if I am expected.

Saturday

It is warm this morning. It will be some time before the sun rises. The desert lies quietly in shades of gray. Stepping out, I examine the other dwellings. I feel eyes all around. They stare at me. Is there some rumor that I am not feeling well? Perhaps I am a curiosity. Maybe they envy me, wishing they were the ones bold enough to attempt such a quest. But what would they know of this journey? Perhaps they only see me as one who has discovered an escape from this place. I wish they did not stare from those gray windows. Quickly, I step forward and the path begins.

I enter the doorway. My eyes rise above me. They take in this mountain upon which I must climb. Repeating the process of placing one foot before the other, I begin. I know how it shall be done. No longer is my attention held to feet or the dirt under them. My eyes wander. Looking about, I see order in the refuse here. I sense purpose or intent. In ways, this place is a reflection of the mountain above.

I approach the ancient tree and its massive pile of leaves. Last night I became part of this pile. It seems much larger today. I continue. The world also seems larger and distant.

Having proceeded along the path for quite some time, I look back and discover that I am not so very far from the ancient tree. In fact, I am within shouting distance. My determination to obtain the summit is made greater by my lack of progress. I recognize points along the path from previous journeys.

Three small stones. Red paper pamphlet—unread. A small, rusted thing. Iron. Narrow path. Small stones, the three down there. Gravel pile. Paper in the tree. Old broken bottle. Sharp green glass. Blood in the sand. Rose in my hand. Three small stones.

I feel shame having allowed my mind to wander and allow my soul to unleave what lies there. To create such images or incantations. I lower my eyes. No longer do I gaze on debris along the path. No matter. Dawn is still some time off. Through darkness, I am unable to see beyond the edge of the path. Looking upward, unable to focus in the black, I realize that dawn may never come. My eyes do not see stars in the sky above. I feel a shroud of clouds covering the mountain.

The path follows one route now. All other tracks do not belong and do not form a part of this path. This is the path which runs straight from the depths of the desert to the summit of the mountain.

The sky becomes illuminated. I approach the small valley of three routes. Without hesitation, I approach the middle route and continue.

The debris here is not unlike the debris closer to the desert. Forest rises up on either side as I ascend. Flanks of small mountainside vales create descending arms of the mountain. They follow the path and rise continuously as I ascend. A flank on the right disappears, giving way to a valley, perhaps a pit. The path circles this valley. Directly ahead, I see the path attempts to cut a niche for itself in the hillside. It appears to go little more than halfway around the valley. Rubble and sand spill onto the valley floor from the failed route. I examine the valley below. The path exits at some point unseen from here. Numerous small routes split away and trail off to the valley floor as the path navigates around the valley's edge. I approach the edge of the path and look down. I estimate that thirty or so fair-sized paces should place me at its bottom. The ground below is flat. With the exception of a large bare tree, crisscrossing paths, and a few blackened spots in the sand where fires may once have been set, this valley seems empty. Descending as carefully as I may, the sand beneath my feet gives way and rushes toward the floor below me. I manage to descend a good distance without having to take steps. I control my downward slide through the sand, and manage to remain upright until I encounter a large stone, slightly covered with sand. My feet shoot from under me and I fall. I throw arms out to grasp hold of anything which might offer support. My hands take hold of air. As I fall backwards, my feet race away toward the bottom and the back of my head makes the acquaintance of stone. Vision fails and the clouded sky above blackens. The rest of me continues to descend this path at a brisk pace. After a short moment, I am no longer aware of where I am.

Coming to a stop, I realize I must be at the bottom of this sandy slide. My vision clears, but I keep my eyes closed because of the pain. Perhaps I have broken a bone. I decide to open my eyes. I begin to stare into clouds, and wonder if I shall remain here with my faculties scattered along the sandy path above me. Maybe I could collect them; put them into my pockets and return home. After some time in bed, I would heal and be as good as new. There is a pain at the back of my head. Certainly this is the point where they all made their unchecked getaway. I am surprised to find that I am able to move my hands and arms. Slowly, I reach behind to examine the hole in my head which must be enormous. My fingers discover only a fair-sized lump where I expected a large escape hole to be. I bring my hand about in front of my eyes expecting blood, though there is none. I turn over slowly so that I face the dirt. After resting for a few more moments, I slowly pick myself up and stand.

And so it is.

I am at the bottom of this place. Gazing around, I try to divine a name. "Valley" is not fitting. Valleys have mountainous walls or are enclosed by hills. This place is encircled by a rising path. This place is an island of the desert which has been cast on the mountainside. This place is not a valley. It is a pit.

I walk about examining my surroundings. I approach a blackened spot on the ground where a fire appears to have been made. I notice many black points where other fires have been set. It is odd others were of the mind to stop and build fires here.

In the ashes I see a few bones. Outside the ashes sits an empty wine bottle. I kick the ashes and uncover what remains of a small book. I bend over to pull the book from the ashes. My head throbs. I examine the burned cover of the book. The fire has erased its identity from the outside. It appears that the center of the book should almost be completely intact with little damage. All of the pages toward either cover are burned severely. Gently, I attempt to open the book to the title page. The page is there, but it is so black that I cannot discern what the title may be or who the author is. The brittle page breaks into bits which fall to the ground. Inserting my thumbs into the book, I slowly draw it open from the middle. The spine cracks and I hold half of what remains in each hand. I drop the right half and examine the left. Poetry. I recognize these lines on the page and yet I cannot remember the poet. Dropping the left half, I look at some of the other black spots in the pit. Without thinking, I count the places where fires have been made. It is difficult to count them as they are arranged without order.

Walking toward the tree near the center of the pit, I pass several spots where fires have been made. Broken bottles appear to be common to most. These spots, which are black with ash, are not bound by stone rings or hollows scratched into the earth. Nearing the tree, I notice the ground close to it is covered in broken glass. Near the tree itself, the ground is so deeply covered that it actually rises slightly. The tree has been the target for many a bottle. Carefully, I cross the glass to the tree. I rap knuckles on its trunk. This tree has no life in it. My knuckles rap echoes of dry, dead wood. I examine the thick trunk. It is missing much bark and is badly scarred from the bottles which have been thrown at it. With both fists, I strike the tree and observe its branches. This tree is dead to its roots. Again, I knock on the trunk. It is amazing that this tree remains standing. I walk around the tree and down the other side out of the glass. When the glass becomes sparse, I turn to look at the tree. The glass pile must keep it erect. My head throbs. I close my eyes tightly and open them again. I pick up an empty bottle. Should I throw the bottle at the tree as others have? Would I help to kill that which is already dead? I set the bottle into the ashes at my feet without breaking it. I wander deeper into the pit, away from where I entered.

I pass many black spots in the sand. Bottles without end. Burnt pages from books, no longer bound within volumes, litter the slopes of the pit. Pages raised to the slopes, perhaps by winds from fires lit here below in an attempt to escape.

I come to a steep slope of rock, a wall it seems, as it is far too steep to ascend by any means short of a rope lowered from above. With the exception of a treacherous-looking crevice in the sloped face, there is no obvious place to descend this wall from above. I step into the crevice at its very base. I tilt my head until I can see the top of this crack. The crevice ascends straight up, making it impossible to climb. I brace myself into the crack in an attempt to use the opposing walls to shimmy upward. The walls crumble under hands and feet. I step away. The air is damp. I hold out my arms. They are cooled by the fine clouds of mist which have begun to fall.

I begin to have a bad feeling. Maybe if I shouted and stomped this feeling could fall from my shoulders and out of my arms. If these rocks do not provide an escape from this place, I shall certainly be caught; imprisoned by these slopes that stand over me. Perhaps my remains shall be freed by some wanderer some years from now. I am afraid of these black spots which litter the floor of this place. So many have gone before. Am I really alone down here? I hold back my head. The rain makes my hair wet. The sky is full and busy. I am glad there is no path. No footsteps to litter the clouds or stars. When it pleases, they fall upon the paths which roam the Earth.

I must get out. Calmly, I walk toward the rocks. I stroll leisurely; there is no reason to panic; I have all the time in the world to find a way out of this prison. Certainly, my fate is not to remain here. It was my own desire to follow the path which dropped me into this hole. My desire, not blind fate.

Upon reaching the bottom of the rock formation, I find that I must sit down in order to catch a breath. I am not accustomed to running so quickly. Looking up, I inspect this formation. The rocks are unusual; sharp and jagged on the top. Yet their faces are smooth as glass. I rise up and spread myself across the face of this stone which stands before me. I hold my palms flat against its face. I press my cheek against the cold stone. A chill spreads through me. It rests. I look up in despair. Perhaps I could build steps, or some ladder, to reach at least some crack that I may grasp and pull myself upward. I gaze around the pit in search for anything that might provide deliverance. There is nothing but ashes and glass.

I lie on the ground in silence for a long while. I no longer weep. I entered this pit deliberately. I would not have done so had it not appeared necessary to pass through the bottom of it. It is obvious that I must return to the path by climbing back up the slope I slid down. I pick myself up slowly. My head has stopped throbbing. I make my way back to the small slope. It is not very high. I turn and examine the pit again, as I did when I stood here earlier. This dirt hole has defeated my quest. I look up the slope. It is formed by a flat stone which offers no foothold or handhold near the bottom. Halfway up the slope appears manageable. This hole has not only defeated my quest, but it has ensnared me. It would be wasted effort to approach the bottom of each wall. I can see well enough from here that all my hopes will not spirit a staircase into the rock or sand.

Without direction or purpose, I wander the pit. I pass every blackened spot on its sandy floor. There are certain places I pass often; particularly near the tree at the center.

It has stopped raining. The air is much cooler. I must get out of this place. It is late in the day. The clouds make it difficult to guess what the time may be, but it is certain to be late. These blackened spots are of no encouragement since I have no wood to burn. I consider the damp tree in front of me. I have no kindling, either. No matter. Even if I had a bit of wood, I have no way of starting a flame.

Without a fire, I am not sure it would be wise to remain on the floor of this pit. If this place is not mastered by some civilized sort, it must be claimed by beast. If there is to be no escape from this pit, then I must take refuge. Looking about, I see no shelter. The only thing other than the flat, sandy floor of this pit is the tree and mound of glass at its center. Though they may be dead, the arms of the tree look strong. They should easily bear me through the night. Perhaps the glass will guard me, though I must lie exposed within the branches. Cautiously, I climb the mound of glass to the tree. I pull myself into the limbs of the tree, avoiding having to return heavily onto the glass in a failed first attempt.

I find myself comfortably nestled in the lower branches. Reclining, I am given a view of the rock formation I earlier failed to scale.

From the tree, the rocks do not appear to be nearly as large or high as they actually are. There also seems to be fewer blackened spots in the sand. When viewed from nearly the same plane on which they lie, the spots were certain to appear more numerous and complex than they truly are. It is amusing that my position in these branches both distorts and clarifies reality. I look to the rock formation and am shocked. Had I only walked to the left of the formation, I could have squeezed between two large stones. Unless my eyes are tricked by poor light, there is also a trail behind them. I had mistaken the rock formation for a stone wall which must be scaled. I laugh at myself; at my inattentiveness. I have spent an entire day trapped in this accursed hole.

I want to leap from the branches, but carefully lower myself onto the jagged mound. At the sand, I dash toward the rocks. I climb around the side of the formation and find that the view from the tree was no cruel trick. I pass between two large boulders which serve as an archway to the trail that lies behind. The clouds have begun to break up. Behind the blackness of the clouds, the sky is dark blue. Somewhere high above this place, perhaps on the summit, it is dusk.

The trail winds about like a serpent through the rocks. There are lesser trails which lead short distances toward smaller formations. Some of these formations have dark nooks; possibly caves. I must return to the path. Often, I must grasp the stones about me to push or pull myself along at high steps in the trail. As I begin to think this trail might be some unending maze, I step onto the path.

I am halfway from the point where I descended into the pit and the point where the path fails. The failed point in the path is not so very far that I cannot examine it before I return to the desert. I ascend the path. After walking some distance, I stop to examine the path behind me. It is difficult to know how far I have come, but the pit no longer lies off the edge of the path. I have passed the point where the path failed. *Appeared to fail.* I begin to descend, and shortly the pit appears. I continue for what distance I perceive must place me at the point where I believed the path failed. There is no misunderstanding where this point is. Where I stand, the ascending hillside is decayed and is nothing but gravel and rock. The larger stones, which have fallen onto the path, appear to have actually been pushed off the path somehow and into the pit. Looking down, I see that the slope descending into the pit is likewise a combination of gravel and rock. I pick a stone from the path and throw it at the pit. As I remove my sight from its bottom, I perceive a dozen dark spots on its floor. For a moment, my eyes search for the tree, which cannot be seen. From somewhere below comes the sharp caw of a bird.

Under the now clear sky, I descend the path. The pit disappears behind and is replaced by forested slopes. The evening sky is full of the moon. It illuminates the path well enough that I am able descend quickly. This full moon plays the sun well. It seems to have been so long since I have seen the light of the sun. Not this evening, day or morning. There was sunlight yesterday, I believe. I do not remember.

The path carries me down the long slope toward the desert. Three small stones. Moonlight reflects off much glass. Much more than when I ascended. The path glitters in the dark.

I stand before the ancient tree and its great pile of leaves. Perhaps I should say something before I finish this day. Something for the leaves. To shout at this decaying mound would mean nothing. Words spoken but unheard. I stare into the black pile and listen to a shrill, distant voice. *Awake! Awake! Fly! Fly away!*

Who says these things? I stand listening. I wait for the mountain to speak. There is no sound. I cover my mouth with my palms. No word has been spoken. I descend toward the dwellings. The wind begins to stir. Behind me, I hear the rustling of leaves.

As I enter the lane my dwelling was built on, I pass the lit windows of neighbors. I approach the dark structure of my dwelling, and let myself in.

Sunday

It is cold this early in the morning. In the east, the sun has not as yet shone her face. Today, I am clad in white. As far as my eyes see in all directions, roofs are white with frost. Above, the sky is clear. A single, faint star hangs in the east. I take a deep breath.

I enter the doorway. My eyes rise to the mountain which lies before me. I stand at its foot. The path rises straight through the mountain. Its crown, the summit, lies naked. One step at a time. One foot follows the other. Always behind. Always ahead.

What is this place? I dare not glance up. From the corner of my eye, I see a great and ancient tree. It has lost its skirt of leaves. Its branches are bare; unable to replenish the mound that once covered its feet. I move toward the desert as it rises into the foothills west of the path. In the distance, I can see one small corner of a graveyard which lies close to the foot of the mountain.

The sun has risen. Her face shines bright. The mountain is sunlit orange and green. I hurry toward the forest and daylight. With the path, which rapidly falls behind me, goes all of the debris I have come to know as landmarks. As I continue upward, I kick a collection of small stones which block my way. They scatter and no longer appear related to one another.

I fix my eyes on the mountain and let the path fall behind. I climb into the arms of the mountain. Slopes rise along side the path. Vales small and large appear, then fade into flanks of greater arms that extend from the mountain. I approach that stretch of path which crowns the pit. I move as quietly as possible. My eyes do not stray from the path before me, and the pit disappears behind as I quicken my pace.

A slope rises to the right and the path becomes steeper. Its curves tighten. There are many empty bottles along the path here. After each bend, I find myself at the foot of yet another slope. The higher I ascend, the greater the number of bottles which litter the path. Looking around on the side of the path and the landscape close to the path, I discover that the only observable debris here is the many bottles which lie about. Few are broken.

The path narrows as it climbs and becomes steeper; its curves tighter. Bottles gradually become fewer. I stop for a moment, turn and look below, thinking I have climbed very high and surely must be close to completing this journey. Maybe with one more stop I can reach the top of this stretch.

I am at a point where the path is so steep that I slide back a step for every two taken. I reach for a large stone planted squarely in the center of the path. I pull myself upward and climb around to its uphill side so that I may stop for a moment and rest. Below, the path quickly disappears into trees. Above, it seems to end abruptly at the skyline. Above this rock, the path is so steep I cannot progress even on my knees. It is now made up of loose dirt and sharp stones covered with the fallen boughs and leaves from nearby trees. An attempt to proceed would certainly send me quickly to some point below.

To the left of the path, the forest climbs upward to the top of this hill. Small trees rise straight upward. Their angle confirms my guess that this slope is not so very far from running straight upward. If I follow the path through the forest, these small trees are dense enough that I might proceed as though on a ladder. I notice a bottle at my feet. Its presence seems strange. I give it a nudge with my foot, push it around the rock, and away it goes down the path. It reaches the bottom intact, then a bump sends it airborne. It shatters as it lands on top of a small pile of broken bottles which have collected at the bottom.

I proceed into the trees. Occasionally, I must step over or crawl under a fallen tree which is larger than the others. Low-lying branches make it difficult to grasp the thin trunks. I grasp at branches. Hand-over-hand, I pull myself forward. Saplings are abundant and provide excellent footing. Uprooting an especially small tree, I scramble to the top of the ridge.

The forest to the right of the path is thin. Blue sky can be seen beyond. As the path bends right, the forest ends completely and the sky opens. To the left, the trees also thin out. Soon, those too, end, as both sides of the path slope sharply downward. The left slope is short, and within a short distance climbs again. This slope rises slightly higher than where I now stand. Its crest parallels the path and converges again with the path further ahead. To the right, the slope drops steeply and becomes mountainside. I proceed along the path as it ascends. Blue sky and the desert plain envelope the right view of the path. I enter a small plateau. This must be the summit. I gaze around, searching for any spot which might be elevated higher than where I stand. A short distance further is a huge rock. Not a large stone lying next to the path, but a huge formation. There is nothing higher. There lies the true summit of the mountain. I head toward the rock, then slow as I approach. It is too large; its sides look like fortress walls. The closer I approach, the greater it becomes. I continue along the path and examine the rock from the other side. I will not give up without having fully examined all possibilities.

I climb down the slope next to the rock wall. I approach the side of the rock which faces the desert below and my hopes rise. Several boulders provide steps upward. Carefully I ascend these stones. I climb up to what appears to be a shelf. There is a crack here in the wall of the rock. Not a small crack which provides handholds, so that I may scale the rock's face, but a full-fledged split I can step into. A door.

I step inside. Sand has filled the bottom of the crack, making a floor. Though the crack appears natural, it seems unlikely that the floor was not provided deliberately. Wondering if there might not be some wild creature inside, I study the sandy floor for tracks. Not observing any, I turn and examine my own tracks. Plainly, my feet lead out of the crack toward the sunlit rock outside.

I walk deeper into the crack, uncertain of what lies ahead. Soon it becomes difficult to see where my feet step. For a moment, I stop to let my eyes adjust to the dim light. I gaze back toward the bright sunlight at the entrance. No longer do I see the walls standing next to me.

Deeper inside, the crack becomes darker. I can no longer see my feet and must feel my way forward carefully. Why am I here in the heart of some boulder atop a mountain? I step forward and bump into the narrowing walls.

Is this it? Does the cave end here? There must be a way to the top of this rock. Perhaps it lies outside. I look up for a moment toward the top of the crack, as though the true summit lay only an arm's length above my head. Cool air meets my face.

I press hands and feet into the opposing walls and push myself upward into the darkness. I raise my arms to feel for someplace to grasp. I find a solid ledge and pull myself up. There is a solid surface where I can set my feet. Slowly, I stand upright. I raise my hands up and discover that any ceiling here is well beyond arm's length. I feel my surroundings. Apparently, I am in another crack which doubles back.

Bit by bit, in darkness, I progress. I discover that my eyes have not yet adjusted to the complete darkness, but the darkness has been broken by light. A few paces ahead and my feet are lit with sunlight which leaks in from a crack in the ceiling. There are more cracks in the ceiling ahead. I proceed, confident the floor will not fail now that I can see it. I pass a few more cracks where sunlight leaks in. The increasing brightness suggests a large opening ahead.

I move toward an opening much larger than that which I had originally entered in this rock. I step out slowly into sunlight and find I am thankful that I did not rush headlong into the outside world. There is no flat rock, no natural shelf here. There is a ledge barely wide enough to stand on. This ledge leads away toward the right of the crack. I look down thinking I might see the stone shelf below. Instead, there are only jagged rocks.

I follow the narrow ledge as it curves around to the outside surface of this rock. It is not so steep that I must climb hand and foot. A few steps deliver me to its top. A small tree has sprouted from a crack in the stone a few paces away. This tree is nearly twice my height, with branches which stretch out and partially shade a pool of water. I approach the tree and examine the pool.

The pool lies within a basin at the highest point of this rock. Its sides are smooth, natural or deliberate. They slope inward gradually. The water is probably as deep as I am tall. Deep enough to be dark near the bottom. The pool is several paces long and wide.

This is the summit. The tree, pool and sky are as calm as ever I imagined. I set myself down under the shade of the tree. Thoughts spin wildly as I lie back and stare into blue sky. It occurs to me; if I were to wait for stars to appear and then the dawn, does this place become meaningful? What if I am now so close to God I no longer have need of sustenance? Is Nirvana a thoughtless gaze of blue sky? Would it torment? Where did this water come from?

I study the pool. Stick a finger into its still surface. Ripples race to its edges. It is freezing to the touch. I stick an entire arm into the water, then quickly remove it. The cold hurts. The pool is so full that immersing my arm caused it to overflow slightly. Sitting here in the sun,

I would think that the water would be warm.

I look down to the path behind this rock and then again into the pool. There is something lying at its bottom. I stare into the water for a long while before I am certain. There is no doubt. At the bottom lies an unopened bottle of wine.

Follow me.

Something Like Jennifer

As I had spent so many years inventing how the girl of my dreams would appear to me one day, I almost missed her entirely. This is one version of the story I sometimes recount for myself when I am alone with a cup of coffee and a bit of quiet music. Actually, it would have been rather difficult to miss her from the start. Somehow, she managed to entangle me in her legs while I was taking my walk in the park. This entanglement did not seem deliberate at the time, since she appeared to be sound asleep at first, but I have since had my doubts.

It is difficult to read and keep a good eye on the path before you at the same time. I suppose that I am, in fact, responsible for our initial introduction. Too good of a book to watch where I was going. I stumbled over her legs as she slept on the grass, and tumbled headlong into a park bench. Apparently, I was quite unconscious for some time, and have virtually no recollection of the event. I have had to rely entirely upon her version of the incident.

Contriving, contrived. I'll wager this tale has something of that odor to it. Sometimes I enjoy a small shot in my coffee, if I suspect thoughts of her are about to begin knocking about my head. It's the dampening effect I enjoy most, especially when combined with a truly strong cup of coffee, preferably espresso. Let's make it a double. Two shots, then, since we're talking double the caffeine.

Meeting this girl, this woman, is neither fortuitous nor unlucky. Fate doesn't exist either. There are times when I'll stare out the window for hours studying a large elm in the yard next door. When I think of her, I ask myself if it is at all lucky for that elm to be so close to the maple which had been planted in my backyard.

It occurs to me that this woman should have a name. Now, if I could choose a name for a woman, any name, I would probably go with something like Jennifer. Yes, a euphonious, good-girl name without all of those seductive *V*s and *C*s, like *Veronica*, who used to live in the house nextdoor. Also, I like the name Jennifer in particular because it has such a sweet-sounding nickname. This is essential for those special endearing moments. Fortunately, I have seldom hoped that wishes were horses; you see, Jenny was a dream come true.

So, we met in the park when Jennifer deliberately tripped me. Maybe I should have been a bit more careful about watching my step, but I genuinely had not expected to encounter anyone as I walked behind the tall thicket of junipers that border the park and concrete drainage basin. I remember telling her that she had picked a peculiar place to be taking a nap. Jennifer was so captivating, though, that I immediately forgot how foolish it was for her to be lying there under the shrubbery.

We spent the rest of the morning talking about life. She was fascinated by how I had come to live where I did at the time. The afternoon soon passed as we painted clouds while listening to children in the park practice softball. As much as I wanted to spend a few more hours with Jennifer, I needed to get home before too long, and so I left her in the park a little before dinner.

The following Sunday afternoon I found myself roaming about the park aimlessly. Inside the pool area, a small group of young children splashed in a circle. A teenage girl in a fire engine red one-piece suit was cheerfully talking to the group, and then dunked her head under the water. I was startled by a cracking sound, and then realized that a softball game was in progress on the big diamond.

A German shepherd sniffed around the empty swings, and then urinated on one of its posts before it ran off toward the back of the park. My eyes followed the dog as it sped across the grass, and the juniper border suddenly grabbed my attention. What were the chances? How could I possibly spend a Sunday afternoon at Toboso Park and not wander by at least once? Except for the pool and ball field, the park was virtually empty.

After deciding that I should take as much time as was necessary to appear nonchalant, I slowly wandered toward the shrubs at the back of the park. Occasionally, I would glance over my shoulder to make sure nobody was observing this gradual progress. I remember thinking how somebody should do something about the gophers. There were holes everywhere. Close to the shrubs, I took one last glance about before I quickly pushed my way through. I followed the border until I reached the spot where Jennifer and I had spent the better part of Wednesday.

I had not actually expected to find her again, and so was pleasantly taken by surprise when I discovered her lying there. She had been waiting all morning. How had she known that I would be there on Sunday? I began to wonder to myself if she had come every day that week to that same spot. At first, I was rather uncertain if I liked the thought of somebody lurking in wait for me for days on end, but then how different was that, really, from something I would do myself?

As I sat down next to Jenny, she asked what I was reading. I had brought along a book, as I often do on my walks. I opened the book to a particularly favored passage and began to read, thinking that she might enjoy this while lying in the sun.

"Ye lofty tree with spreading arms,
The pride and shelter of the plain;
Ye humbler shrubs, and flow'ry charms
Which here in springing glory reign!"

After reading only these few lines, she begged me to stop. She said the language was unbearable. Looking around at the low-hanging juniper branches, she declared that the lines alone sounded horrific.

This comment made me wonder what Jenny possibly could have done for a living that qualified her to be such a critic of literature. She claimed to be a waitress at the diner just outside of town on the interstate. Nothing really. The position of waitress seemed much too farfetched for me to believe. I had already spent enough time with Jennifer to recognize that here was a woman of refined character. I believe she was, in reality, a prominent socialite who did not wish to be recognized. She was young enough, in fact, to be a local debutante. Of course, I did what any gentleman would do; I permitted her the anonymity she obviously desired, and questioned her in this matter no further.

I spent the remainder of the afternoon detailing for Jenny the history of my career to date. While describing a particularly significant yet lengthy incident, it occurred to me that I was certainly becoming boorish, and so I changed the topic to something which might seem a bit more interesting to her. At least I changed it to something we might have more in common. Following a brief discussion of "serial" literature, Jenny insisted that I return to the topic of my career. She was primarily interested in hearing accounts of my more remarkable successes.

It was around six o'clock when my lady and I said goodbye. I stretched my legs as I worked my way out of the shrubbery. It was the first time in hours that I had stood up. The pool closed at four o'clock and the large ball field was now empty. Looking around, I noticed that the only other person in the park was an old woman sitting on a bench near the sand play area. She was facing me as I had come out of the shrubbery, and so I decided to pass by close enough to bid her good evening.

As I drew close to the old woman, a large growling dog came running at me from the field behind her. It was now dark out, but the field lights had come on, and I recognized the German shepherd I had seen earlier in the day. I stopped for a moment so as not to alarm the dog, and held out a hand for him to smell. I wanted him to see that I was really quite harmless. This appeared to intimidate the dog, who instantly switched from growling to barking. When the old woman called for the dog, it stopped barking and moved to the her side.

The old woman apologized for the dog, but then quickly defended its behavior. She said that she often felt vulnerable when she went outside of her apartment alone. For her birthday some years earlier, her daughter had given her the shepherd as a puppy. As a Christmas gift the following year, she sent him to obedience school, and then for a few weeks of attack training.

Perhaps the thought of another birthday passing, or just the talk about puppies, upset the woman; it looked like a tear was rolling down her cheek. I may have been mistaken about this since it was, at this point, quite dark now, and only the lights in the ball field remained on. Believe me, I felt little satisfaction knowing that I was correct about that tear when the old woman shook lightly for a moment and then began to sob freely. I asked her what was wrong, but she only muttered incoherently. I quickly decided that she was probably not in her right mind.

I asked if she was going to be alright or not. She waved her arm in the general direction of the play area, the swings possibly, and mumbled something about her daughter. The old bat was obviously not a well person. I asked her if she needed some help getting home. She wanted to know if I had seen her daughter.

This woman was definitely *not* right. I suddenly realized that she had one of those wire baskets on wheels that you see old people pulling behind them everywhere. Maybe she was homeless. Reaching as deeply as I could into my pockets, I grabbed as much change as I could fit in my hand while still being able to get it back out. Thirty, maybe forty Mercury dimes flew onto the grass as I passed the old woman and headed for home. From the street, I could hear that mad dog barking wildly.

The next morning, I planned to pass the park on my way to work, secretly hoping I would be able to catch a glimpse of Jenny. A block away I glanced at my watch. I had left early that morning so that I would be able to spend a few minutes by her side, if I were lucky enough to find here there. Arriving at the park, I discovered a small crowd of police cars and an ambulance in the parking lot. Police were roaming all over the field as though they were looking for something. I wanted to tell them to watch out for the gopher holes, but then figured they would see them just as well as I had. One officer was awkwardly climbing about in the children's play equipment. It definitely did not look like anyone was going to be taking a peaceful stroll with such a ruckus going on, so I thought it was unlikely that I would be running into Jenny that day.

It was a couple of weeks before I was able to find enough time to get over to the park again. Finally, one Wednesday afternoon, I came by for a walk. I was reading a new book and was having some difficulty becoming involved with the characters. I found myself skimming over lines without really reading them, and often flipped pages while not being quite sure if I had actually finished them or not. Thumbing through a volume in this manner, I found myself behind the junipers wondering if there was any chance of finding Jennifer there at all.

When I drew close to where Jenny and I met, I heard voices and then a bit of giggling. It seemed strange to hear voices here, so I hesitated for a second. Then, as silently as I could, I pushed my way closer to the giggling voice. I was surprised to find two young boys under the lower branches. One was lying on the ground motionless with his eyes closed and his tongue sticking out of the corner of his mouth. The second boy, who knelt on the ground next to him, giggled wildly at this scene.

As I took another step forward, the boy who lay on the ground opened his eyes and stared wide-eyed for a moment. Before I knew what was happening, he jumped up screaming and dashed out of the shrubbery with his friend close behind.

Appassionata

It takes many seasons to form my thoughts. It is only after the passing of more seasons than may be counted that I realized that I once had a life. A life outside of the world which I exist in. Of this life I have no memory whatsoever. Well, that is not entirely true. I do remember clearly those very last moments as I fell.

I have no memory of a childhood. No memory of a mother who never baked yet read to me every story in every book I managed to latch onto. No mother to hold me and wipe the tears from my face. Tears of small childish thoughts. Dreams broken by the reality of grown-ups and grown up things. No memory of the time she cried and refused to let go of me because I must become part of that grown-up world.

I have no memory of a sister or two brothers. It would be both difficult and easy to be the youngest of four. To follow in the footsteps of Excellence, Chaos and Apathy. To follow, that would be easy. To measure, this would be difficult. Leave me alone. I follow no one. No remembrances of a dominant brother who desired to forge my thoughts by pulling me through knotholes many sizes smaller than my frail mind might wear. I do not know of brothers or sisters.

Would I remember my father? If only I could! I wish I could remember those times we shared together, he and I. Long hours, or perhaps days, sitting at the edge of the ocean, watching the tides come and go. Would he ever have told me that he loved me? Perhaps I never had a father. Abandoned to be raised by my mother, sister and two brothers.

I have no thoughts of a best friend who knew me well enough to anticipate gestures, words and thoughts. A friend who, in time, stepped aside and observed as my life unfolded and folded. A friend who probably sits in the darkness watching and waiting.

There is no sweet face or blue cotton dress that smiles to me from the green grass under a large shade tree. Oh, her face! Her smile hurts my heart and makes it both cry and sing. No other eyes have touched my soul like those in that smile. Her laugh, a sweet rain which echoes that voice. I miss her whispers. I do not remember, but I feel.

I remember falling. I have no memory of the precipice. Only the sudden shock of awareness that I was no longer standing with my feet firmly beneath me. The flailing of my arms to regain my balance. My mind raced back into the earlier years of my life and desperately searched for salvation. Words. The correct thoughts, quickly before the gravel below becomes the rocks beneath my body. A chant, a prayer. "I have fallen, prepare to sleep, should I die . . ."

I never believed that God has an ear for me and me alone, or that God holds open a palm for each thread in the fabric we make. Would God offer a closed fist to the good, the innocent? I do not believe God is listening.

If I calm and feel backward, I can recall my sudden arrival upon the rocks. It was quite shocking. The sensation of impact was deafening yet silent. Like a dream. I became instantly both blind and deaf, and though I could not breathe, the hitch in my chest and head made me smell and taste blood mixed with the soil my face was likely buried in. Only a moment, and all thoughts slip away. As they do, the world around me, though I can barely sense it, expands to dimensions beyond my comprehension. Though my ears cannot hear, there are the fading sounds of a methodic beating or whacking within my head. The world no longer expands. There is no more sound. All is quiet and I know nothing. Calm is sudden and complete. A far greater calm than any sleep. I still sleep, but I have learned to dream.

I dream of a body broken upon rocks below a small cliff. I dream of slipping away from that body. Not out of that broken shell, but in it and away from it. The ground beneath that body is cold. The stones which lie around it seem colder still. I feel from these stones. I feel an odd flickering of warmth from the sun, along with a stinging chill. I know this chill is the cold of night. It is calming to feel the sun warm the stones and the moisture in the soil. *Why the flicker of warm and cold?* Perhaps my senses are slow and the night and day pass so quickly that I perceive only a flickering of both. Perhaps only the small bit of rock and dirt which lie under this body cannot feel the sunlight. *Do I actually sense this?* Perhaps my body feels these things and my mind is confused. I feel the flickering upon the back of this broken body. I know this to be sunlight. Time is not right, this is certain. I feel this body warming in the sun. I sense decay in its heat. I sense this body leaving bit by bit. I realize now that it is reducing greatly with every warm flicker. I do not only perceive those rocks which lie beneath this body and the soil between them. I sense more. I feel myself spreading, slowly reaching outward. I sense a large rock and many more smaller stones. I feel all the soil and the sand which connect them. There are small dead branches here, and here. These are lighter and sense the flicker of warm and chill differently, somehow less severe.

Everything is still calm. I feel the flesh of that body is now gone. I feel the flickering of warm and cold upon my bones. Calmly I reach. If I concentrate upon the flicker I sense it slows for me, so that I may perceive it more clearly. I try hard, and feel that it truly is not a flicker but a throbbing or rhythmic pulsation. If I feel for it, it makes me remember what it was to breathe. Drawing air in and then letting it out. Somehow, I feel sunlight being breathed in while moonlight is exhaled. And then the sunlight is exhaled and the moonlight taken in. The Earth is buzzing.

I calm as I spread and reach. In all directions more stones and soil. And here, a small distance from those bones, I feel something which grows. If I feel, I can sense this growing thing reaching upward, balancing in the air. Leaning into the warmth as the world throbs into sunlight, and then twisting about in the moonlight to lean into the warmth again and follow it as it moves away and leaves. A cycle of gyrating with the sun and moonlight. If I feel harder, I know that this grows with or without the sun. It gyrates with or without warmth, but it dances to the sun, which makes it tingle, healthy and lean. The soil buzzes. It breathes. It feels.

I calm into the warm. The Earth, my face, soaks the sunshine. I feel it warm. I calm. Time stops for me. I remain in perpetual sunshine. Ages pass as it slowly moves across the sky. I cannot see it, the sun, as it slowly progresses in its journey across the sky, but I feel it. The passing of a single day. I calm and time stands still.

Something steps into me. Some creature of intent, whose light footfalls thunder across me and cut a path as it stalks. It hunts. I gasp as I lurch forward and swat that which grows but no longer gyrates under the warmth of the sun. I tingle. I gasp as I lunge. I tense. The world stands still for a moment, and I pass that small plant and look beyond the small rock to pursue whatever I saw quicken and escape to its other side. I stalk forward. Vision fades as I move away. I do not control these feet. I calm, yet the world begins to flicker.

No longer do I feel a buzzing. The world is both dark and bright. The more I calm and feel, the more I see and sense. So much. Thousands of eyes. A multitude of hungers, and feeding. The Earth, she will not give one without demanding the other. No death, no food if there is to be no sustenance, no life. There is no death. I calm as I pursue and surrender. I sigh. The Earth is happy. Life pulsates warm and cold as I reach, slowly.

There is so much within this valley. So many needs and desires. We fear the cold of night, for it has become cold even during the sunshine; and I have died, and fed. With many eyes, I look with varying degrees of understanding. I know of man, the one that walks so loudly that I must hide. I know that I must flee from any that do not hop, fly and seek small seeds and crawling things, those things better poked up from under the soil. I think of places, and know this valley and the stream with fish which lies beyond the large stones. I do not feel this stream, but I know it. Life is warm and the world pulsates. No longer must I reach. I am calm.

Seasons pass. Sometimes they die, and I weep when I am not strong. The cold time takes many. It hurts to watch those die, yet I feel no suffering when I am gone. It is fortunate and contenting to find the windfalls of those who no longer suffer and have surrendered to the cold. We shall survive to the spring and then it shall be warm.

I wish I had some recollection of life before the fall. Some memory of what is now the past. I do feel guilt knowing I was once a man. This I know. It is difficult to think. These thoughts have taken seasons to form. I know of arms, of walking and speaking. I know of mothers and families, the things important to people. Thoughts have come, and I know of the divisions of men and women. I have come to remember. I cannot remember my life. I feel.

Awareness of the world around me no longer spreads and reaches outward. I have felt from every corner of this small valley, but I cannot reach beyond its boundaries. There is no desire to. I am at peace with all that dwells and passes through this place.

Seasons pass. With and without eyes I have learned to feel and see the world around me. This entire valley I now know well. Every creature, though I hold a multitude. Every flower, weed, blade of grass and seed, unfulfilled. Every stone and the dark moist which hides underneath. The sand and soil. The river which runs through sand and rock, the small fish. The lake which lies far beneath the surface where the sun cannot reach. I feel it all.

Still calm. There is a new thing in this calm. Awareness which floats beneath the cold face of the moon. I calm, darkness remains suspended. The fabric of being begins to pulsate with starlight. Melodious thought drifts toward dawn through air. Vague feelings of humming too difficult to comprehend. Too perplexing, no matter how long I calm. Slowly, warmth from the sun surrounds me. Then a moment. A hard shine from that face spreads over me. Hot light pours into every corner. In this moment, as though I have caught fire, I feel a beautiful and terrible eruption. Immediately, I know music. This is no mockery of strings or winds, but a pure thing. A pulsation which makes me laugh because there are no ears. I am carried off as though I am a lullaby. Awareness slips into harmony. Into slumber. Now that I understand, I know that I can rest.

Time passes. I sleep in the warm sunshine. I bask in the starlight. It is glorious, the snow and sunshine. Seasons flicker.

Awake! I feel as though I am slapped. Shaken from this slumber, my soul cringes under the footfalls of man who is here. Who is now. Not the footfalls of a man, but the thunderous steps of a woman, barefoot. Repeated unaware, shocked by the sudden appearance, dodging and hiding from the silent slithering which the very air screams. Perfumed air which is not of flowers or meat, but the lure and tension of some toxic aroma. Sweet and violent. Why this molestation? Leave! There is nothing here; we have all hidden and shall not come out until you are gone and that scent goes in the wind.

She tarries.	*So warm this stone.*
She stops, and sits.	*Only a moment, to sit.*
The wind stills.	*The wind quiets.*
The valley stills	*This valley so calm.*
in her presence.	*So sad this place.*
I feel.	*I miss you.*

Her footfalls thunder over this face as she slithers away in the chaos of thought. Her memories hover in the air, and then flutter away in the breeze, along with the sweet fragrance which falls from her as she dances off. As she mounts the small, unused man-path, the one which ascends around the unwarmed wall that climbs straight upward, there is laughter. Her bare feet step off this face and she is no longer felt. This footpath ends feeling. Her presence is no more. This fragrance stirs my memory of life, stretching slightly more into the past than the fall. That sweet voice so close to my ear—sweet secrets. Her warm hands on my back—I was shocked by the push.

A sweet rain. So warm this stone. The Earth sighs, and I forget.

The Death of Peter Rabbit

Andie had forgotten to buy eggs with the rest of the week's groceries. Shortly before noon the Friday before Easter she left a message asking me to stop by the market. This was certainly enough of an excuse for me to call it a day early. Shortly after lunch I headed off to pick up a couple of dozen before heading home.

April was unseasonably warm. The three kids spent the better part of that week swimming in the doughboy as though it were late August. It was our second year in the Shadow Hills house. Long enough to have learned how predictable warm weather can be. With sixty-degree winter days, year-round pool service was inevitable.

Shortly after we moved to the three-quarter acre block of land, the children decided we should adopt farm animals. Preferably a horse. Certainly a pig. To their dismay, their mother and I settled on rabbits: Flopsy, Mopsy, and Peter; rats: Jack and Jill, and a mutt we call Chucho.

Pulling into the driveway, I had expected to find the kids still splashing about in the pool or sunning themselves on the back patio, red-eyed with chlorine. I was somewhat surprised by the sight of the three of them sitting in the middle of the flower bed at the back of the house. Marie was in her ballet skirt, and Gregory's Nutcracker outfit was covered with dirt. If it were any other day, I might have investigated further. I was determined, however, to jump into a cool shower and let Andie deal with the situation of ruined clothing.

I am not sure what I had expected to find Andie in the midst of once indoors. I don't suppose that I really know what Andie does with her afternoons. I found her in the study reading poetry. She was reading aloud to the photograph of Frida Kahlo hanging over her desk. The window was open and I could hear the children outside singing songs they had learned from their aunt in Santa Fe. *Little Bunny Foo-Foo*. Gregory gleefully slapped Marie in the back of the head every time he sang the verse about the field mice. Marie's ears turned bright pink as her temper rose. Fortunately for Gregory, they took up *Here Comes Peter Cottontail* before she bloodied his nose for the third time that week.

The children were in the middle of a funeral service for Peter, who had been found dead that afternoon. The ceremony was held next to the blackberry hedge in the flower garden, but apparently I was to bury Peter close to the vegetables once they had finished.

"It may have been the heat," Andie said, looking away from the window. Gregory was throwing pebbles at the shoe box coffin Marie had decorated with daisies.

Putting off showering until after dinner, I went to the shed and grabbed a shovel. As I pulled back on the first bit of soil, Andie called the children in to color eggs.

As usual, Chucho was chained to the apple tree located midway between the house and the back fence. While his chain is quite long, it still manages to keep him from reaching both the bulbs in the flower bed at one end and the rabbit hutch at the other. As Peter's grave became deeper, Chucho kept his chain taut and sniffed at the growing pile of damp soil. A couple of times he scratched at the dirt and then jumped back with a bark. When the hole was nearly three feet deep, it was time to fetch Peter.

Even though the pile of dirt was going to be put right back on top of Peter, I had dug the hole as straight-walled as I possibly could and just wider than the width of the shovel. It appeared much deeper than it actually was. It looked at least six feet deep as I balanced Peter's shoe box on the pile of soil. Chucho immediately grabbed the box's lid and tossed it into the air.

After retrieving the lid, I discovered that the box was too large to fit into the hole. My first thought was to smash its sides in until it would fit. Perhaps I could push it to the bottom with the handle of the shovel.

I could stomp it down with some soil on top. The image seemed brutal, so I merely removed the lid and dumped Peter's carcass in. He had apparently died spread out on the floor of his cage and was stiff in this position. Peter did not fit neatly on the hole's bottom. I had imagined him curled up as though sleeping. Instead, his eyes were wide open as he did a lopsided headstand. I pushed him to the bottom as best I could before filling the hole in.

Once the final shovel full of dirt was stomped level with the rest of the ground, I took a large stone from the pile behind the hutch and covered the mouth of his grave. Chucho barked wildly as I carried the empty shoe box off to the garbage can.

On weekends, the kids generally wake up several hours before we do. Friday evening Andie deliberately kept the kids up well beyond their bedtime in the hopes that in the morning we might have tea, coffee and read the paper without interruption. On the way to the kitchen, I closed their blinds and turned on the cooler, thinking this might keep them under their covers for a little while longer.

On the counter next to the coffee-maker was an open bottle of lime juice. In the dirty sink water, its green plastic cap floated like a little boat. Andie can't drink tea without lemon and honey. For a moment I considered capsizing it. I'd play stupid later when she asked where it went. As though it really mattered, I wiped off the cap and put the fruit-shaped bottle back into the refrigerator.

"Out of lemons?" I asked, sitting down to the breakfast table. Andie wrinkled her nose in disgust as she sipped her tea.

"I forgot to have you pick one up with the eggs. This stuff is nasty. I think I put too much in." She grabbed the honey and filled her cup as much as her one sip allowed.

"You know," I said staring out the kitchen window, "it really wasn't that hot yesterday."

"Yes it was," Andie snapped, adding another sip of honey to her cup. I could tell she was beginning to sway into her weird space.

"Listen," I said, "the water bottle in the other rabbits' cage was completely empty. Peter's was half full when I got home."

"I don't know!" Andie said. "Okay, *okay*, it wasn't the heat. I found Peter impaled to the bottom of his cage with one of the cue sticks from the kids' table top shuffle board thing."

"Caroms game."

"Whatever. Anyway, he tore up his paws trying to reach his water."

"So what did you do about it?" I asked.

"What did I do about it? I don't exactly know what happened. Do you?"

"Oh, I can take a guess."

"Don't you dare! I told the kids rabbits don't do well in the heat. We probably should have kept him on the patio. Besides, they had fun getting dressed up and all. Did you hear them singing? I'll get some goldfish next week."

From the kitchen window we could both see Chucho in the backyard straining against his chain. He was trying to scratch his way closer to the stone covering Peter's grave.

"I wish he'd stop that before he hurts himself," Andie said, dropping the empty honey bottle into the trash.

I watched Chucho jump against his chain as Andie rummaged though the cupboard. He was actually making the branches of the apple tree shake.

"I think I'll go by the feed store later. Do you want me to get the kids another rabbit while I'm there? Flopsy and Mopsy still haven't had bunnies yet," I asked.

"No," Andie said, "Besides, we'd probably end up with another reluctant breeder. I'll pick up some goldfish Wednesday."

"Reluctant breeder?" I asked.

"Sure, remember when Marie brought Bugsy home from school? Peter went wild when I put the two of them together. Marie's teacher couldn't have picked a better name for that rabbit."

This was news, and yet it made perfect sense. Marie had once said that Peter preferred strange bucks over Flopsy and Mopsy. She had asked several times if we could get another rabbit. She would name it Benjamin, and then maybe Flopsy would decide to have some bunnies.

The children love stories. We read to them constantly. Marie loves stories with animals like those in our yard. Rabbits and mice, for the most part. Gregory likes fairy tales. Andie will read to him from Anderson or the Brothers Grimm. He wants tales of witches or fairies, because stories with animals or pets often keep him awake or cause him to have nightmares.

As the morning wore on, Andie and I drifted off in separate directions to take care of a variety of incomplete projects. As she disappeared in the direction of the garden, I headed toward the study.

It was later in the afternoon when I spotted Gregory wandering about the backyard with a heavy load of something in his T-shirt. Standing next to Chucho's tree, he began to shout for the dog to sit down. Chucho is part coyote and is almost completely wild. He is quite intelligent, but has, at times, seemed too stupid to train to stay or play dead, let alone sit. Gregory has no patience whatsoever, and stomped his foot to punctuate the command. I was amazed when Chucho's ears perked up and then he sat down as instructed. Gregory immediately rewarded the dog with what might have been a bright green ball he had been carrying about in his shirt. Chucho tossed his treat into the air. I recognized the crack of a hard boiled egg as it landed at his feet. Obviously, Gregory had found the colored Easter eggs in the refrigerator and was planning on feeding them to the dog.

My mind was elsewhere, and so it took a few moments before it occurred to me the boy needed to be stopped. I was still staring out the window with coffee in hand when Andie dashed out of the garden and pulled Gregory away from Chucho's reach. I would have expected stern words and maybe a timeout. Instead, Andie transferred, one at a time, the eggs from his shirt to her blouse. Before returning the eggs to the kitchen, she gave him a little wave, indicating that it was time for him to skedaddle onto something else. Once Mom was gone, Gregory dashed back to the still-sitting dog. Grabbing both ears, he pulled their heads together and kissed Chucho on the nose.

After dinner, the kids wound up on the back patio playing cars. Between Gregory's violent crashes and Marie's overly dramatic cries for help, I was going to have to close the study window if I wished to have at least one coherent thought. As I got up to crank the window closed, they seemed to drop their game of commuter traffic for a bit of quiet talk. At the mention of eggs, I thought I just might leave it open for a while longer.

"I saw you giving Chucho our eggs."

"I didn't," Gregory said.

"Yes you did, I saw you from the garden with Mommy," Marie said.

"Oh yeah," Gregory said, aiming a tractor-trailer in the direction of the rat cage, "why did we make so many?"

"For hiding."

"Well, I didn't want Chucho to lose any then," Gregory said.

"They're not for him, they're for Easter," she said angrily.

"I know, but I don't want Dad to lose them in the bushes," Gregory said, pushing the truck back and forth trying to build up speed.

"Those eggs are supposed to be for us!" Marie said.

"They are?" Gregory said, seemingly amazed. He let go of the tractor-trailer, sending it off toward the rats. Like a baseball pitcher, Marie threw a tow truck into its path, hitting the semi's tractor squarely in the side. Gregory erupted with crashing sounds as truck parts flew in every direction. Marie began to wail for help. I got up and closed the window.

Ten minutes later, there was enough shouting outside that I couldn't think, even with the window shut. Through the curtain I saw Marie giving her brother a shove.

"He did not!" she screamed.

"He looked like he was gonna bite me," Gregory yelled, shoving her back. "I'm glad he's dead!"

It was time for the kids to go to bed.

△

Easter morning. The kids began their search for eggs in the flower garden. Using Chucho's bowl to hold his eggs, Gregory searched frantically in the hopes the others would find few or none at all. Andie and I drank coffee as we watched from the patio. We laughed when

Marie snatched three eggs from Chucho's unattended bowl as Gregory crawled deep behind the blackberry hedge. She dashed off toward the other end of the yard before the missing eggs where discovered.

"He's gone!" Marie cried, standing on the large, overturned stone next to the vegetable garden, "Peter's gone!"

Just then the neighbor's cat ran out from under the blackberry hedge and jumped over the fence. Gregory was close behind, stick in hand.

"Stop that!" Marie shouted, "Let Peter go!"

As soon as Gregory saw his mother and I get out of our chairs, he dropped the stick and started in with how rabbits are *really*, *really* fast. Especially Peter, he added. Looking at the upturned stone, Gregory thought that Peter must also be *very*, *very* strong.

Peter's grave was indeed empty. I still don't know how Chucho did it. Andie's eyes suddenly grew wide. She was watching him gnaw at a furry bit of something that had apparently once belonged to the dead rabbit. She distracted the children with news of breakfast as I quietly removed Peter's foot to the trash can.

The children discussed Peter's escape from the grave as they sat around the kitchen table eating stacks of pancakes. Gregory suggested that Peter might not have really died in the first place, and so obviously slept for two days before digging his way out. Marie, however, was certain that Peter had been quite dead. "It wasn't the sun that killed him," she said "I saw myself that he was stabbed with a carom stick."

"Fire before smoke," Gregory added.

"That's for starting the game," Marie said with a look of disgust.

"Well," Andie said smiling at me, "if Peter is alive, then it certainly is a miracle. You kids must certainly remember the time Peter narrowly escaped the toolshed from . . ."

"No, no, no!" Gregory cried. "I want Hansel and Gretel. Cook the witch!"

It was at this point that I sent the kids back outside to look for the rest of the eggs. Andie lay down with a migraine while I picked up a little in the kitchen. She only needed about thirty minutes to shake enough of her headache to see again. She blamed it on too many chocolate eggs.

Rather than go out into the bright sun, we decided to watch the kids from the study. They finished their hunt for eggs and were hard at work on the chocolate eggs Andie had put out.

"Mom said it *was* a miracle," Marie said.

"You know what?" Gregory said.

"What?"

"You know what Peter told me before he ran away?" Gregory said standing up. Nobody said a word, and so Gregory continued. "He told me he's never coming back again."

"He did not!"

"Did so," Gregory said.

"Well, you know what he told me first, then?" Marie said jumping up. "He said that if we're good, he's gonna come back and bring us a surprise."

"He did?" Gregory said with a puzzled look on his face.

"Yes! And he said he is going to be watching *you* lots." She pushed him into the hammock.

The patio was silent for nearly a minute. While Marie finished the remaining eggs, Gregory swung in the hammock and seemed to study Chucho.

"Marie," he said, staring out into the backyard.

"What?" she said without looking up from the candy dish.

"Do you think rabbits' feet are lucky?" Gregory asked.

Dylan's Child

That initial sense of panic gives way to mere anxiety as my search along the river's edge begins to drag on without result. I doubt whether, in fact, I only imagined hearing a death groan. *Death groan.* Silently I work my mouth to form those words. I laugh to myself when I think of how this must sound. I try to imagine repeating this later. Repeating it at home.

Like the mystic Nile, the Conway river runs south to north as though it had no sense of this Earth at all. Here, near this section of bank, it murmurs with a sad voice. This strange voice may well come from the sea. I clear my throat and feel as though I'm not even significant enough to be ignored. Staring into the water nearest the bank, I try to remember what this groan must have sounded like. I have forgotten already. Perhaps nothing more than a phantasm of the steady flow of water. A distant groan, hard to imagine now. It might be best if I were to recount it more as a cry of distress, or perhaps nothing more than a grunt.

A sudden gust of wind blows up the river's course. I turn my face aside and study the empty cottage for a moment. I had neglected to take a look at the well that sits just behind it. A sense of urgency washes over me again as I fabricate in my mind how that voice may well have come floating up from some dark hole in the ground. It's a struggle to resist the urge to dash toward the well.

Whispering into its depths, I wonder if anyone is here. "Hello? Is anyone there?" A small stone falls from my hand, and instantly clacks on the stones below. This well is not so very deep. There's an old wooden bucket at the end of a frayed length of rope lying on the grass. I nudge this with my boot, uncovering bare earth underneath. The number of worms squirming about between the bucket and soil seems strange.

As the breeze slowly drops off, I begin to imagine still more voices. As I return to its banks, the murmur of the river grows louder. I notice a strange bit of weed floating near a stone just under the water. A hand floats to the surface, and I realize that this "strange weed" is, in fact, long black hair streaming off a head, bobbing just below the river's surface. Stepping onto the stone, I reach down and grab a handful of this hair and pull the attached body ashore before the river takes it away and offers it up to the sea.

A heavy, dark wool dress is twisted around her legs and stuck to the rest of her like a thick wet skin. Pale lips are drawn back in an unsettling grin as her unblinking eyes stare into sky blue nothing. Too much like a landed fish for me to stay long at all.

Heading back to the cottage, I think of how I should find someone in the village to come and collect this sea foam woman. Slowing near the well, I reach into my pocket. With barely a thought, my fingers close around a small silver coin. It had been given to me by my father when I was a young child. I stare at a small circle of stones and try to imagine who it is I should actually bring back from the village. Perhaps I shouldn't bring anyone. I'd rather not become any more involved than need be at this point. I've never laid eyes on her before, yet I cannot help feeling responsible in some way.

Before I realize what has happened, the sound of the small coin tings from the bottom of the well. This is immediately followed by several squawks, and out from the well come two, no, three black birds in a confusion of wings and flight. Rather than disappearing into the distance, these birds perch on the roof of the cottage and begin to sing loudly. There is movement in the corner of my eye, and I am astonished by the sight of my recent catch slowly crawling her way back toward the water. I dash back to the river's edge and fall to my knees next to her, interfering with her return to the river.

Inside the cottage, it is only slightly warmer than the riverbank. It is, at least, out of the wind. At one end of this cottage's single room sits a large rock next to a stone hearth. I examine the cold ashes and wonder how long it has been since anyone has slept here. There is no wood at all for a fire. I eye the woman, still wet, as she crawls across the dirt floor of the cottage into the far corner. It would be worth the attempt to take a quick look outdoors to search for a few scraps of kindling, possibly a branch or two.

After a quick look around, I discover there is, in fact, no fuel at all to be found close by. Some distance upstream, there is a stand of trees on the river's opposite bank, but too far off to be of any use now. I return to the cottage.

"Are you all right?" I sit on the cottage floor facing the woman. She stares through me, unblinking. I wonder if she is able to speak. Some time passes, a few minutes perhaps. She looks a little too much like a flounder again. I draw near, thinking to touch her, to make sure. Her hands clench tightly at her side. Looking at the stone wall behind her, I try to think of what I should say. I've spent so many years rehearsing the proper words. I hadn't anticipated this at all.

"I don't suppose you were expecting anyone, were you, Viviane?" At this, she stops looking through me and locks her eyes to mine. I'd have guessed tears, given the situation. Rather, I'm surprised her stare is dry and angry.

"I'm sorry," I say. Her stare does not waver. "I've interfered here, I can see that." She releases me; lifts her eyes to the dark ceiling, and draws a deep breath as though it were her first.

I had always felt certain I'd find her one day. There have been no words at all between us to confirm what I've always believed. That angry gaze was evidence enough. Still, it is not as though I was the only one to have ever taken up this search. My quest, however, began where most of the others dropped off. Hunting about what should have been her home in Arantes turned up nothing at all. It had seemed so right that there should have been something, and yet there was nothing at all. I became convinced that Egerton Sykes must have known more about her than anyone realized.

Were it not for Mr. Sykes, I don't think anyone could have even imagined a connection between Viviane and Dylan ever existed. The idea of such a relationship seemed so preposterous to me, that it almost didn't occur to me that she would have actually followed him to this place.

But, of course it didn't occur to me at first. This is why I spent so much time looking for her in all of the wrong places. All of the "wrong" places had been investigated many times by all those other fellows. I knew this, yet I repeated all of the same mistakes. Other than a great deal of lovely countryside, there was nothing to be found at all.

Suddenly, I realize that I've been rambling thoughtlessly. Maybe not, I'm not sure. Looking to the woman, I realize that I'm quite uncertain if I've been speaking these thoughts aloud or if I might not have only mumbled the odd word. Many years I've spent with my mind full of her. Too many years spent alone, obviously.

Her eyes lower slightly from the ceiling, and then slowly drop to meet mine once more. No longer colored with anger, they don't seem intent on imprisoning me. These eyes are open and speaking. They are plainly sad.

"Interfered," she whispers to herself "yes." Her mouth smiles lightly with these words, yet the eyes remain unchanged.

"Forgive me," I say, "please understand that I still believe in you."

Slowly her smile spreads, becoming huge. For a moment I'm elated, knowing that I must have certainly touched something. This elation lasts only a moment, then I am stunned by a burst of laughter. This laughter is disconcerting in its obvious lack of joy. She is laughing *at* me. Her laughter tapers off quickly as she runs her fingers through her knotted hair. She grabs a handful and pulls it across her eyes.

"Believe in me? Why should you?" She lets her hair fall and stares through me once more. "What of all the others? They stopped believing in me ages ago. The couple here and there who pay me any thought at all have no idea who I really am. To tell the truth, I don't think I mind, either. The pathetic tales those fools have made up are better than being remembered as some kind of whore."

"Nobody ever thought that . . ." I've absolutely no idea what she's referring to.

"Nobody, really?" she asks.

"You must be thinking of some story I've never heard. And that's fine, because I'm not sure I'm prepared to deal with it. I found you. This is what matters."

"Yes, and it's your fault that I'm still here. Let go." She clasps her hands together and holds them up as though she means to plead.

"You were already here. It's not my fault at all." In my opinion, if she should be blaming anyone, it ought to be that Sykes fellow.

"No, it's his fault. Had he never written what he did, I wouldn't be in this place," she says, glaring around the empty cottage.

"He?" I ask.

"Yes *Him*. You've no idea how many souls he's made miserable with that ridiculous book of his."

"But he's dead, and I'm the only one that knows you're here."

"Then it is your fault. You see, you still believe in me," she says, hands open, palms facing toward me. Pleading doesn't appear to be an option.

I must say, this was an idea I'd wondered about when I was younger. Perhaps she has been a prisoner for all these years. Could that really be my fault? All of those years searching, I imagine I should feel terrible. I hold out a hand, to let her know how sorry I am, but realize she's gone. She's taken her opportunity and left the cottage.

Outside, she stands next to the well. The river seems quiet, as though it were listening.

She turns away from the well, looks at me with a smile, and rests her hands on top of her head.

"I had a cellar dug recently," she laughs, swaying her hips lightly. She almost dances as she moves closer.

"Really? Where is it?" I ask quickly, glancing between swaying hips and the well behind her.

"On the other side," she gestures for me to follow with both hands as she begins to wander around one side of the cottage. "Come, I'd like you to see it." On the opposite side of the cottage, there is a boulder lying close to the cottage wall. Viviane pushes it to one side with apparently little effort. This seems frightening somehow. She touches me lightly with her fingers, and before I can pull away, my hand is in hers.

"After you," she indicates a small hole in the ground.

I look into the darkness, and laugh. I think to myself that she can't possibly believe I would attempt to put myself into such a hole.

"But of course you shall," she whispers.

I look at her in hopes of not offending. This hole is no cellar. She smiles and then kisses the back of my hand. "Please, get in." I try to force a laugh, realizing that she is serious, but discover I can hardly draw a breath.

From over the roof of the cottage floats an odd bit of bird song. On the other side of the river, shadows from trees seem to grow night. This is more of a cave than a cellar, really. Somewhere above, in the closing starlight, the river groans like the rhythm of sea waves.

The Matinee Somersault

Paul Linderman was six years old when his father decided, apparently without warning, that it was time to pay the circus a visit. Paul's father had never heard of *Cirque du Peser* before, when on his way home, he saw a billboard advertising that this troupe would soon be in town. Since he had never been to a circus before either, he wondered if this might not be the *real* circus. Luis, a man in the factory where Paul's father worked, said he knew of them. They had passed though Toledo once. They had a first-rate show as he recalled; their acrobats and clowns were the finest he had ever seen.

As Paul spends his inheritance throwing loaded softballs at aluminum milk bottles, his father takes in the sights outside the Big Tent. He watches in amazement. The whole thing seems too much like a county fair somehow. The midway is filled with local riffraff and small children. Everywhere he turns there are circus people in threadbare outfits. Many, like the fellow setting up Paul's bottles, seem to constantly have a cigarette stuck into one corner of their mouth. He squints so he can see while setting up the bottles with both hands.

Paul loves cotton candy, so his father is willing to let him wait in line while he sees if he can complain to anyone about the prices in the concession stands. He had never seen five-dollar hotdogs before. Once, at a baseball game, Paul's father had spent two dollars for a foot-long wiener, but never five dollars. This was robbery disguised as—well, he wasn't sure what it was disguised as. He wants to let somebody know that he would have felt better if the hotdog guy had held a gun to his head—because then, he would have *known* he was being robbed.

Behind the restrooms, Paul watches a well built man hammer away at a large box. This man has all of the white clown makeup on his face, but none of the funny clothing. What is it? Paul wonders about the box.

"A casket," the man answers, then begins to attach hinges for the box's lid. Paul wonders what a casket is exactly. He once heard his father say he needed to buy one for his car.

"A gasket probably," the man says. "This is a casket for a funeral. You know—to bury somebody in. I used to be a cabinetmaker when I was younger. I gave it up to join the circus, if you can believe it."

Paul watches the man attach the casket's lid, but mostly he looks at the picture of the clown on the man's bare arm. It looks like one of those deranged bad men on the covers of comic books. Circling this clown's head, like a halo, are the words *Loco Payaso*.

"See that?" the painted man says looking at the clown on his arm, "It's because of him I'm not a flyer anymore. No tattoos allowed the boss says. I'd have to fly in sleeves, I guess. What that really means is that I'm off the trapeze for good." The man sits down.

"I'm Tony," he says, holding his hand out for Paul to shake. "I suppose you're here to see the trapeze act or maybe the elephants."

What Paul had really hoped to see were the clowns. He had never imagined he would be talking to one halfdressed and building a box to bury somebody in.

"I'm glad you're here to see the clowns," says Tony. "Now, let me see," he says snapping his fingers, "that's why I thought it was a good idea to be one. I like to hear kids laugh." Paul wonders if Tony had suddenly remembered why he became a clown, or if he had just made this up.

Paul's father is upset to find Paul far from the line he had been told to stay in. He doesn't like the look of Tony, either—brown and sweaty, sitting next to Paul. When he grabs Paul's hand, Tony waves goodbye and gives Paul a wink. Paul and his father wander off toward the animals.

Paul's father had hoped the circus would have some sort of petting zoo for children. Instead, the animals are mostly dangerous bears and felines. All are in cages with warning signs and seem dangerously accessible to even the smallest of children. As it turns out, the only animals they are able to see up close and touch are a few of the elephants.

While waiting to ride the elephants, Paul listens to his father talk to another man in line. The man says that when the elephants are not in the ring, they are put in tiny travel cages without enough room turn around in. And if they are not performing or giving kids rides, they are shackled by two legs. Some, like those giving rides today, are dying of tuberculosis infections. The man says he thinks that maybe the circus is going to start some kind of epidemic before moving on to a new town.

Paul doesn't know what tuberculosis is, but he is sure that what it means is that the elephants are sick. Paul believes this, too, because elephants are supposed to be really big and sort of fat. The two elephants everybody is riding, Mattie and Joy, they don't look so good. Paul rides around the small corral on Joy's back. He thinks the elephant breathes funny when she walks. Even though she moves slowly, Paul is afraid. He wonders if Tony will have to build a gasket for her pretty soon, too.

As Paul and his father wander outside the Big Tent, Paul begins to think that the people who live at the circus are most likely gypsies. He watches a man with a tall black hat pull birds out of the air. Paul is thinking the clowns are probably magic, too, because Tony said he knew how to fly in the air. Paul's father had seen the bird's white tail up the magician's coat sleeve, and is convinced they are all a bunch of cheats and swindlers.

While his father haggles at a ticket booth over the price of the show in the Big Tent, Paul dashes back to where he saw Tony the clown work on the box. There is something he wants to ask him about flying clowns.

"You know, I'm not really a clown yet," Tony says, putting the final touch on a flower he is painting on the casket's side. "Tonight's my first show, and as you can see," he says indicating the casket, "it'll also be my last. The boss didn't just pull me off the trap, he said I'm out of this *Circo de Pesar* completely. He said that if I like clowns so much, then that's how I'll go out."

Tony explains to Paul that the casket is a prop for his first and last show as a clown. There is to be a pantomime of Antonio's supposed last great flying act, and then a funeral in the center ring. He used to be one of the star fliers. But not now. The boss said they will draw huge crowds if a rumor could be started about how the troupe's top flier fell with no net during a matinee performance. The only catch is that they never did matinee performances. The boss said it didn't really matter; crowds of people will come anyway.

Paul and his father sit just inside the entrance of the Big Tent. Paul tells his father that he wants to sit in the middle, close to the center ring. His father says that the tent is going to be full of people soon, and he wants to be able to get out quickly when the show is over. As people gradually enter in twos and threes, Paul watches the vendors dressed as clowns, but without the makeup, circle below and shout at the people in the stands.

Popcorn! Peanuts! Cotton candy!

Finally, at the far end of the tent, Paul is sure he sees a clown with real makeup. He looks like he is throwing something to the children in the stands. Paul pulls at his father's sleeve, begging to go to where the clown is. Paul's father is busy watching people wander in slowly. The show should begin any time and he is surprised there aren't more people. Paul lets go of his father's sleeve and dashes toward the clown, who is now headed toward a large man in center ring.

Near the middle of the tent, Paul sits on a ground-level bench. The clown is talking to a bald man with a mustache and huge arms, who is digging some kind of hole in the middle of the center ring. When the clown sees Paul, he skips over and throws him some candy. Paul asks if Tony the clown is going to come. The clown smiles and bobs his head up and down wildly, *yes*, then dances away toward a group of clowns near the tent's entrance. Paul waves excitedly for his father to take the seat next to him.

Paul's father studies the dancing clowns and their strange wool and linen outfits. He wishes his son had remained near the exit. He expects it will be a short performance, however, so he decides to let the boy enjoy himself.

Suddenly, music fills the air and decorated ponies ridden by glittering ballerinas stream into the tent. They circle the tent twice, then the smallest of the ballerinas rides to the center ring and takes off her glittering dress. Everyone gasps when the dress falls to the ground and then laughs when they see that this dancer is actually the ringmaster. He is wearing white riding pants and a black top hat which makes him look taller than he really is. Paul thinks he might be the same man who grabbed birds from out of the air.

The ringmaster asks for ladies and gentlemen, girls and boys to listen carefully. All about to witness the most amazing show touring this part of the country or presently anywhere else in the world. There will be high-wire acts, clowns, animals of all kinds; yes, elephants! and more. Now in the far ring, for all to see, are seven dancing bears that will amaze everyone later in the show, and in the ring nearest the tent's entrance are the world-renowned *Clowns du Peser*.

In the center ring, as all can see, Bruno, the world's strongest man, is currently at work at the most solemn task ever undertaken at this or any other circus. Bruno is digging a grave.

The volume of the music drops slightly and the ringmaster's voice rises. It is here he makes the sad announcement that this afternoon, during a rare matinee performance, the famed trapeze artist, Antonio Zuniga, fell to his death, here in the center ring. He attempted, bravely and without aid of a safety net, the only known attempt ever made at a quintuple forward somersault with a triple twist. The ringmaster shouts that it must be known, that to the credit of his troupe, Antonio accomplished this very feat before striking the ground. As a tribute to Antonio, this evening's performance will begin with a reenactment of this last great flight.

Clowns begin to circle the center ring on red and green bicycles with off center wheels followed by a miniature fire engine covered with still more clowns and orange paper flames. As they circle the center ring, honking and waving to the spectators in the stands, a safety net is lowered from somewhere above. The ringmaster announces that one of the clowns shall impersonate Antonio. His daughter, Maria, will assist this brave "Antonio" to the rope which leads to the trapeze.

One of the clowns riding on the screaming fire engine is tossed off into the center ring, where he stumbles on his oversized feet and falls face down into the ring. Paul recognizes Tony, who is brushing dirt from his trousers at the same time a young girl in a red sequin dress dashes into the center ring and stands on tip-toe to give her father a kiss on the cheek. The ringmaster waves his hand toward a rope ladder, then steps to one side as the show has already begun.

The girl in the red dress takes hold of Tony's hand and leads him, wobbly-legged, to the rope ladder. The clown plainly appears to be afraid of heights. This causes him to frequently misstep through the ladder's rungs, feet shaking in the air. Each time this happens, he looks down fearfully. He lets go of the rope for a moment and holds his hands in a pleading gesture. Paul thinks he can read Tony's lips as he gazes toward the Big Tent's ceiling, *Please don't make me do this . . .*

As Tony nears the top of the ladder, the girl in the red dress laughs loudly. She is at one corner of the safety net and is sawing at it with a knife. She stops momentarily to hold one finger to her lips as if to ask everyone not to tell. She smiles at Tony, blows him a kiss, then continues to saw at the net.

High above the center ring, Tony is on a small platform, unaware of the girl in the red dress and her surprise work on the net below. He hugs a pole and looks around wildly as though searching for the quickest way down. A trapeze is swung into the air and Tony lets go of the pole and moves close to the platform's edge. Below, the girl in the red dress cuts through one corner, then dashes off to the next, laughing.

Though the clown's legs quake in fear for all to see, he spits in his hands then rubs them together as he eyes the swinging trapeze. Paul believes Tony is not really afraid and will decide to leap quickly. The clown does leap, but screams as he does so, arms flailing. He catches the trapeze by one hand and releases himself on the platform atop the opposite pole.

"Mama!" he cries, arms spread wide. The girl in the red dress cuts through the second corner. As the net falls to the ground, she dashes off to another corner. The crowd below laughs.

The clown catches the trapeze as it returns and leaps from the platform, his legs running through empty air. He lets go of the trapeze and falls toward the center ring. The crowd cries out, but the clown is caught just above the floor of the center ring by a small trampoline-like net mounted to a pole. He is launched back to the highest trapeze where he swings for a moment, legs jerking oddly, then falls again. On his way down, the girl in the red dress cuts at the last corner of the big safety net. Clowns in the center ring pull the fallen net to one side. Tony springs from the trampoline again wailing this time as he does backward somersaults toward the ceiling of the Big Tent.

The clown repeats this fall five times and on the fifth fall, instead of being launched skyward again, he manages to slow himself suddenly and do a little back flip onto the floor of the center ring. He lands flat on his back, arms and legs shaking in the air as though in pain. Clowns gather around and then leap back as a large red and white daisy does a sit-up on Tony's chest. *Antonio the flier is dead.*

As the clowns wail and mourn, Bruno, the strong man, marches into the tent with Tony's casket thrown over one shoulder. The clowns lay Antonio's body carefully in the open casket, and the ringmaster says that even though it is a sad day, they still have great things to look forward to. It is his pleasure to introduce to the show Antonio's third cousin, Paulo, who will take the great artist's place on the highest trapeze. High above the center ring, a strong young man does a triple somersault over a newly raised safety net.

Paul watches the clowns below wail as they drag the casket to the open grave. The loudest of them, a fat fellow with a derby and green hair, reads from an open book, then squirts the tall clown reading over his shoulder with the flower on his lapel.

When the casket is lowered into the hole, Paul sees Tony try to scramble out of the box. Paulo, the strong young trapeze artist, leaps to the ground and hits Tony squarely in the head with a shovel—*ping*! Tony slumps back into the hole, and Bruno leaps in with a hammer. The crowd high in the stands watches him as he nails the casket lid closed.

Paulo starts to shovel dirt into the hole even before Bruno climbs out. In a flash, all the clowns are shoveling dirt alongside Paulo, and in a moment the hole is filled. As the clowns ride off on their bicycles and fire engine, Paulo helps the girl in the red dress onto the back of Joy, the elephant. She joins Mattie and the other elephants as they dance about the center ring, breathing loudly and spitting blood.

It was the first time Paul's father had laughed all day.

Setting Fire to the Tent

The Weed

Spring and waking.

I remember early one morning I had a thought.

I had a thought and then I took a stroll out of the front door. A quiet little stroll. Well, maybe not a stroll; it might have been a bit more like a slow creep. So I sneaked down to the driveway. Just to have a look. Not that there was any particular reason to be sneaking about at six o'clock in the morning. Why should I be the one to feel like a thief? It was just one more Saturday morning.

The air was not bitter. Strange, I remember how my mind was preoccupied with books and papers filled with numbers which covered the dining room table. I had no business being out there in the sunshine. What I really needed was a good hard slap to bring me to my senses. Why, inside there was another pot of coffee probably ready, certainly waiting to help me face round six.

On the way back inside, I stopped for a moment. Out of a narrow crack in the walkway, a bit of green caught my eye. It seemed so terribly odd to see a little sprig of green poking up out of the middle of the walk. I really had to stop for a moment to admire this determined little thing. There, sprouting out of that crack, was a weed. A weed just like the ones in the backyard that had put up such a fierce battle last fall with a dying lawn. Crowning this weed, here in the middle of the walk, was a tiny white flower.

I do not believe that I had ever expected to see spring again.

I knelt there on the walk. I think I may have become lost in the sunrise or perhaps in the wet soil covering still buried tulips. Lost for a moment.

Sunset and evening.

I think maybe what I needed was sleep.

Outside the bedroom window the streetlamp brightened for a moment and then snapped off suddenly. This temperamental light had been behaving like that for over a month. I kept expecting someone to complain and then the city would come and fix it. I had hoped that it would be left unlit. Outside the bedroom window there was a dark new moon. I put my face to the cold glass and stared into the shadows that ran along the cinder block wall. Without the streetlamp, stars shone on my home. I lay down and closed my eyes.

Morning and grieving.

I was surprised that I woke at all.

Sunday morning lying in bed. They are all in church now, I think. What was that thing last night anyway? It was a dream, wasn't it? I thought it rather unkind to interrogate me like that. Questioned in the middle of the night. Certainly a dream. No sane mind would ask such ridiculous things at such an ungodly hour.

"Do you think you could look into his face and survive?"

"Do you actually dare claim to know his mind?"

Oh, what nonsense. For God's sake, turn off the light!

So here I am, sitting, shuffling about bits of paper and staring at some more numbers. I wonder if that really was just some disturbed dream. Maybe I should go out front and stare into the sun some more. Then there is this thought which keeps going round and round in my head:

> *Neither fallen rocks nor mountains shall hide you from the face of him that sits on the throne.*

I think, "Great, this is starting to get biblical. I know, I could hide. I could just walk away from it all."

So I do, I walk out. I walk down the walk a short way. I am standing here and I am thinking. I am thinking and then I ask myself, "Am I not a man?" I look down and catch a glance of green under my heel.

Over the Wall

Just the other day I happened across something peculiar as I was digging through the mahogany box that sits on my dresser. Women have jewelry boxes; what do you call it when the box belongs to a man? Jewelry box, does that sound silly? The one pair of cheap cuff links lying there hardly qualifies as jewelry. Perhaps the jewelry is that collection of bright brass padlock keys I keep buried under a stack of business cards I stuff in there in order to maintain an orderly appearance on the dresser top.

Let's see, something peculiar. I was digging through the box trying to locate that spare gas card, which I had not signed yet, when I found this small red stone about the size of a quarter. I immediately recognized this little red item. It was a carnelian pendant I had given my ex-whatever shortly after we first started dating. I suppose the word "dating" is a complete misnomer, an affair was actually what we were having at the time. At any rate, here was that little stone pendant. It was the first thing I had ever given to her. As I recall, the last time I saw the thing, she had just ripped it off of her neck and tossed it into the kitchen garbage.

Everything and anything that had to do with that woman I have long since thrown out or burned. Even the cheap wedding band she had given me. Oh, that was a tough one. First I had hammered it flat, then I took a pair of tin snips and cut it up into a half-dozen little pieces. Then I threw those bright little gold chunks down a storm drain. As ridiculous as this might sound, the entire operation was performed rather calmly, since I despise spiteful and ridiculous behavior.

So there lay this little pendant. How did it end up in my jewelry box, I wonder? She used to wear it on the end of a thin little gold chain. That chain, however, became history when she removed it that time in the kitchen. Here, in my jewelry box, this pendant had a long black thread strung through its gold loop. I picked up the pendant and examined the thread. It looked like silk. The knot tying off the thread was rather curious. A double fisherman's knot. Now, that woman did not have the brains or the dexterity to tie such a knot. Could that be done accidentally I wonder? I squinted my eyes to look carefully at the knot again. There was no way it could have been tied that way by chance.

Burned wedding pictures and smashed china are a long time in the past now. I have quite gotten over the bitterness that had consumed so much of me at the time. This pendant, though, it definitely needed to go. I had little desire to hold on to keepsakes reminding me of the largest mistake of my life.

So here I am, staring out the sliding glass door of this little apartment. This stupid little red rock has got to go. Simple enough; cross the carport, a quick hop and I am over the cinder block wall that borders the apartment complex driveway.

Here, on the other side, there is a dirt path which cuts through the neighboring dirt lot and up into the desert foothills that lie to the south of my apartment complex. This dirt path runs pretty much uphill as I proceed away from the parking lot.

The sun is low on the horizon, and so I quicken my pace in the hopes of reaching my destination before it sets. As usual, it has been rather windy all day, and the air is full of dust. The setting sun appears almost red as it glares through this filthy air. The dirt path before me, which is normally just light grey sand, appears a warm orange.

Behind a low formation of hills in the distance, the sun slips. I stare at the sharp shadows which lie around me as they slowly lose their definition and gradually become one. I raise my eyes to the sky and begin my search. I seek the first.

From behind, a gust of wind blows over the hilltop. A sheet of dust suddenly blinds my eyes. Thoughtlessly I swing the pendant on its string as though I were about to slay Goliath. The stone flies. An impetuous cast, a misdirected toss. The damn stone has shot straight up.

High above I see a bare speck as it hurtles skyward. There, in a sandy gust, the relic is caught. And there it goes. It flutters away into the desert. In an instant, the stone disappears into the distance, sailing over juniper and Joshua trees. Lost now for good is that little gem.

Oh, how rash! There are no stars, not one. I had so wanted to make a wish. So I shall sit down here in the sand to wait. Finally, high above the horizon, there is a little white pin prick. A faint hole in the shade. Perhaps I shall be held accountable for damages.

Star bright, I have thrown away that old heart. I take back the words. All those wishes, which were nothing more than lies.

After a few silent minutes I stand up and brush the dust off my jeans. As I quietly return along the dirt path, I pass a large white rock which lies a short distance away off the path. I wander off the path and kneel down to have a look. Actually, this rock may not be as white as I imagine it to be. It is a little difficult to tell in this light. I pick up the stub of some small branch and begin to scrawl in the sand.

Silently I trace images. Letters and then words. I trace my desire. I scrawl these things deliberately yet hastily. Hastily before this desert wind whispers tales. Tales which may betray me. Betray this heart.

Carried by the wind from some distance, I hear a faint shouting. This voice comes from the other side of this small hill. Quickly my feet obliterate these glyphs that I gouged into the ground. I would rather there were no evidence.

The path home is short. As I approach the cinder block wall, I stop for a moment. A sudden memory holds me. I take a deep breath. Strange, these thoughts have nothing to do with that pendant back there or the woman it once belonged to. She could never be one I could ever truly love. My thoughts are somewhere else. They are so many years away. Now, there is the memory of an embrace. The image of a sweet smile. I force another breath and wipe away a tear.

This wall I leap.

Antediluvian Music

I'll not bother to check the fuse box. Notes continue to float through the door and away into sticky night air. The sky over the horizon is orange and indigo. My feet spot a river's disguise. It is a strange desert evening when small waves lick your toes. An odd sort of creature swims by, shaking its head. On the cinder block wall on the other side of the stream, an old friend beckons for me to cross over. Inside, lights snap back on and notes fall silent.

In the March Hare's Library

A rumbling.

From another room, the sound of running water. A flame has been lit. I stumble about thoughtlessly, aware only that I am my own captor. I slowly push my way through crowded furnishings, stand next to the window. I pull aside the curtains, stare into blackness.

A pair of worlds mirrored in the shadowy calm of slumber. Sleep filled with faint stars. Newborn thoughts topple from some high place, fall from some filmy pinnacle which is not sleep. A place without shadow, filled with brilliant moonlight.

I am aware of two worlds. I must be only half as wise because of them. I am a child. With a laugh, I roll a ball, toss a note. On a table before me, a menagerie of small toys. A wild gathering I alone have created. Like a small child, or perhaps a god, I pick up a small red ball in one hand, a green one in the other. These two worlds are about to collide.

The calm.

In another room, rolling water falls silent. The teapot is about to speak. Caught somewhere between this place and that, I pitch into consciousness. Catch myself before I sway too far and fall entirely out of this reality. Grab hold before I tumble headlong into some other place, maybe some other life.

Here, a pair of eyes are mirrored in the nervous shimmer of dreams. Dreams filled with hidden smiles. I sway about uncontrollably, stagger senselessly out of these dreams. I watch the clock on the wall; it spins trying to find its own time.

A typed page floats in the air between us.

I sense those eyes and gaze indifferently into some book because of them. A bit of crumbled up paper falls from heaven to the table before me. With a slam of my fist, I find a page. Break a spine. With a stolen glance, I place palms on ears and pick up a pen with my teeth. Before I begin to pound my head on the wall, I glance over. Desk to desk. I glance over, realize that half of a story is about to begin.

A scream.

From that other room comes a muffled bang. The teapot has begun to shriek. No longer caught or swaying about wildly, I have fallen completely as though thrown. Cast off from that other place and dropped into this. I fall like some weary tree shedding its leaves.

Here a pair of lives mirrored in the bright calm of a deep pond. A pool filled with exotic fish. Feelings floating up from some deep place glide about on the white caps of waves. Feelings foamy as clouds drift to this shore, and discover a chilled autumn afternoon.

I feel the drawing of these two lives and must believe there is some mad bliss because of them. I am just a man, for goodness sake. A ripe blue tear falls into my words. An open book before me, thoughts bleed together. These thoughts begin to swirl about until I find myself knee deep in a blue pond. I cannot swim, I must wade through thick water. Wade to the edges which lap on a shore of white sand. I stand on the shore's edge, stare into the deep water. I watch as fish swim about wildly and know that here there is a story which has not yet been written.

The silence.

Quick, look out the front window. The tea is on the table.

Phoenix

Thursday evening concert. I close my eyes for only a moment because that is how I see the night air best when I am here. Despite crossed beams of light, a single engine hums overhead jealously vying for my ears. An impossible distraction. In the seat behind me, an old man fumbles with some plastic store bag which should have been lost earlier this evening. I open my eyes, they have become surprisingly heavy. A young couple sneaks through the curtain and sits nearby. My eyes close. Quietly. I find that after several days with little to no sleep, it seems rather difficult to discern the difference between the rising and falling strings of Stravinsky's *The Firebird*, and the cool night air which felt so fresh against my face. Still closed, yet I know that this is exactly how the night air looks.

I drift slightly. My thoughts begin to wander. Thoughts of firebirds. What sort of bird could this could be? Still closed, I see an oriole in a birch tree. I wonder if she could be the firebird. I remember a child's book, *Are You My Mother?* I begin to wonder, if I concentrate a little if I could not recall some other bright feathered creature which might live close to my home. Notes rise high, perhaps this is a bird. I think of her and I become uncertain whether I dream.

An image of some magical firebird reappears. Still closed, I think of some page where I might become enlightened, yet all I can find is *Fisher King*. Peculiar indeed, a kingfisher would be understandable, but *Fisher King* makes no sense whatsoever. The entry seems vague. I can only make out something about a grail, whatever that might be; and then, "see *Waste Land, The*." I now know that this could only be my imagination, because I recall once being told that one cannot read in dreams. Something about the wrong side of the brain.

But for some reason, some strange reason, it all begins to make a kind of good sense. Good strange sense. Death by water. So I selfishly think of this heart. I try to recall a forgotten poem. It almost seems ironic that I walk this earth only because of a dozen poems and three hundred pages of supporting documentation. Saved a dozen times from the flames myself. Grown so large, it seemed a child I had given birth to, like a hermaphrodite, some twenty years ago. Children should not play with matches. *Chance* caught fire a fortnight ago. Death by fire. Yes, it all begins to make wonderful sense.

That was two weeks ago and midnight. A small oscillating fan two feet away became enormous. My eyes closed, still closed, I consciously tracked its progression up and down my naked body. The breeze on my toes was as light as on my nose. Another night with something better on my mind than sleep, perhaps better than dreams. Lying there alone while this brain, two days elsewhere, seemed so lonely. I thought of her and was uncertain whether I dreamt. Finally, I just couldn't stand it any more. I had to get up. I had to do something constructive. Perhaps something destructive. I slipped into a dark closet and dug for two boxes which held the remains of something which had been bothering me for some time. That evening's diversion was three hundred pages, handwritten, and all the party favors which tagged along. Bright kitchen lights came on and the tea kettle was set to work. Within an hour that thing, that creature, was dismembered limb by limb, page by page.

The tea kettle was set to work again. Another hour, it was quartered and filled a tall plastic kitchen trash bucket. Now it was beyond saving. And then, after nothing else was left, I set flame to the single bit of scrap paper which had come first. Those first few words which had started it all. The birth certificate. I stared into the flames and could not help but feel that I should have been stopped somehow. The phone never rang; God never called. I often wonder if Abraham had been nothing more than a coward. Death by fire.

I jerk forward knowing that I have indeed dozed off, though only for a moment. The orchestra has become rather noisy. I cannot bring to mind any firebirds that would ever consider a home in the desert. I look at my feet and wonder if there could ever really be a phoenix.

Beyond Geometry and Allegory

With too many things on my mind than must be good for me, I pace about in small circles. As I sometimes do, I create these small circles wearing nothing more than threadbare thoughts and finger-locked palms on my crown. Somehow I should know better, though. My thoughts are of her. They are of walking away from this place. To live on a farm in the mountains, perhaps near a shore.

My circles become tighter. Nietzsche said to step beyond.

I close my eyes and wonder just whose son I might be really. It is just that it seems that I do not understand the “ins” and “outs” of reality. Or sin. Maybe this heart, this blood, maybe it cannot reach beyond yesterday. I have no ancestors beyond father or mother. Somehow I have been missed and so am ignorant of right and wrong.

The telephone rings. My circling stops and I become a point in time. I pick up the receiver. The message is brief; you shall be missed.

I have become fixed as a point. I have become lonely here. Naked, wearing only palms on my skull. I am lonely in my ignorance. I make my decision. From the bowl on the counter I grab a piece of fruit and wander off to get dressed.

A Day Without Mail

As I wander along generally aimed toward the mailboxes, I think about this entire business of dreams and reality. As I walk along a concrete path, my eyes thoughtlessly scan the busy parking lot. My thoughts are of you. They are of yesterday and wild places that seem to exist only in my imagination.

"You're a sick man."

If this were truly meant only in jest, then why do their eyes seem so sincere? I cannot help myself or stop these thoughts from weaving in and out of this place any more than I can stop the laughter which is born out of the confusion I see in their eyes. Why do they laugh along if this is insanity?

I have come to realize that their life and mine transpires on different worlds. They yearn for madness rather than lay dead eyes upon the reality of this place. With this one good eye, I should exile the lot of them, offer myself a boon. I am intoxicated with you as I lay a hand across my mouth and dig into a pocket with the other searching for a mailbox key.

At the interchange, I steer toward the freeway that leads north into the desert. I glance behind me, and look at the setting sun. Somewhere, ten minutes behind, we kissed goodbye.

Double cappuccinos and a bookstore parking lot; I wonder if these are the things or just the pseudo-reality I love to puzzle over. The road behind is empty. I enter a new lane as the road widens. I pass lanes to the right. All are empty. The sun slips behind low hills somewhere in my rearview mirror. I hold a finger to my lips, smell desire.

I peer inside the mailbox, which is empty. This does not disturb me, really; I have been captivated by yesterday's goddess. She sits with an outstretched hand gripping the hair on my head. With her other hand, she covers her eyes. I am surprised by this image of her sitting before me. As I lay eyes and fingers to such beauty, I feel certain that I am blessed. Perhaps I would blush if these words were spoken aloud. For a moment I stare at a bare white neck and whisper to myself, "Here is my goddess." I look at the open palm which she holds up like a mask. I wish that I could somehow stare through it and into your eyes.

In sandals, I stumble through torn up asphalt as my thoughts dash along on an empty highway away from you. Where is here? This may be more than a rational mind can make sense of.

When I walk through sand, I measure large circles wearing Levis. I measure small ones here, in bare feet as I grasp for still more fruit. I search through drawers, frantically searching for a box of matches. I turn off the lights and close my eyes.

Water Fowl

M: The path leads away to both the right and left. A feather is not a scale nor a chicken egg. I wonder if there is, in fact, any reality for those things in the past for which there can never be empirical proof. What is reality? I look at sunflowers through the plate glass windows of a dress shop. I wonder why not a sequoia. Why not a German carp or a pair of chicken lips? Does it all boil down to marketing or aesthetics? Were I to look through the correct plate glass window, I might, in fact, catch a glimpse of a rainbow trout swimming about a one hundred percent cotton extra large. If you crossed a Rhode Island Red with a Mallard what color eggs would I eat for breakfast?

K: But it isn't the inside of things that you ever see. You see the outside. You see the color of my eyes; but the inside of my eyes is gray, especially if I am about to die, which I may be, you really don't know. The outside of the whole relationship thing is often very pretty, they'll have bread makers and coffeemakers, and they'll have enough kitchen equipment that, well, it seems clear that they're making it, but they aren't inside. The whole thing has become who first began to refuse to sleep with whom, who first let the baby get a diaper rash, who insisted on turning on the bass while Mozart was playing for the guests. You don't understand the rottenness of it all.

M: Are questions or wonder a failing? The failure to understand . . . Why not a dandelion? It is round and yellow. That would seem close enough. I thought you told me that size really wasn't important. You can eat a dandelion just as easily as you can a sunflower. A carp as easily as a trout. In China they prefer carp. A cultural delicacy. Smoke and mirrors. So many words, and what it is that I actually ponder over is; how is it that a scale becomes a feather? Those things we cannot see or prove becomes anyone's guess. Primordial soup may well have been lentil soup without the hamhock. Everything is prehistoric to a chicken. Yesterday and the Golden Age of Greece are not so far apart. For myself, it is difficult to distinguish between last year and the Sun King's twentieth birthday party. I wonder what today will become.

K: You wonder, you wonder, I cannot believe you spend so much time wondering. Make something. Make a fire. Make a woman go crazy with desire, make a book, make a book happen for yourself. You will only feel the Sun King's wrath if you do not become the Sun King. You get lost between reality and this dream state. Please understand that the only way a pot of soup was ever made was because someone decided to put in ingredients. I am adding you to my life to create fire. I am writing to create magic. You snake your fingers along my wrist. What are you doing? You say things will work out. Work them out. I am creating a poem. What are you stopping me for? I was just at the point where the painting had begun to run out of the bathroom. I believe in paintings as sentient beings. Do you? I am a dandelion. I have eaten yellow lips. I am washed with celery water. Evolution begins with me. I am creating yellow celery with lips. I am creating wildness in you.

M: Dreams are, reality is . . . *I am*. I could build a fire or imagine myself as Sun King, were it not for the fact that I once shined that boy's shoes. Perhaps you think it sad that I could ever have been a regent's shoe shine. But think of it, on the memoirs alone I could make a fortune. Trust me, it wasn't all butter and brass polish. I think I would like to travel to Wales. Northern Wales—across the strait from Anglesey. I would like to travel to Wales and write a book. Perhaps something about how a god from one time somehow becomes mixed up with a goddess from another. A brief collection of twisted little tales. How many would be required for the effort? Sixteen? Nothing to it really, I suppose.

One, two buckle m' lord's shoe.

It would put me in tears.

The Fire

At first it seemed like only a dream. Choking back what should have been a laugh, he grabs a red votive from the mantle.

Tent flaps catch flame.

Exeunt ravens.